INSOMNIA

RAVI SUBRAMANIAN, an alumnus of IIM Bengaluru, has spent more than two decades working his way up the ladder of power in the amazingly exciting and adrenaline-pumping world of global banks in India.

He is the author of ten bestselling books. His first book, *If God was a Banker* won him the Golden Quill Readers' Choice award in 2008. He won the Economist Crossword Book Award for *The Incredible Banker* in 2012, the Crossword Book Award for *The Bankster* in 2013 and the Raymond Crossword book award for *Bankerupt* in 2014. His books have been translated into Hindi, Tamil and Latvian.

He lives in Mumbai with his wife, Dharini, and daughter, Anusha.

To know more about Ravi visit www.ravisubramanian.com or email him at info@ravisubramanian.in. You can follow him on: Twitter @subramanianravi and Instagram@ravisubramanian70.

JIGS ASHAR is an award-winning writer and banker-turned-consultant. His first short story, *The Wait is Killing* was adjudged a winner by Jeffrey Archer in the *Times of India – Write India Season 2* contest; and his second, *Make(up) in India*, chosen by Shobha De, was also a winner in the same season. His third story, *Duel*, was shortlisted for the *Juggernaut Short Story Prize* for the year 2018.

After nineteen years with leading MNC banks, Jigs took the plunge into writing after getting a certification in Creative Writing from Xavier Institute of Communications. He currently works as a consultant with the World Bank Group. He is also an avid marathoner.

Jigs lives in Mumbai with his wife, Vidya, and daughter, Esha.

You can follow him on: Twitter (@JigneshAshar1) and Instagram (@jigsashar).

RAVI SUBRAMANIAN
JIGS ASHAR

INSOMNIA

First published by Westland Publications Private Limited in 2020
1st Floor, A Block, East Wing, Plot No. 40, SP Infocity, Dr MGR Salai,
Perungudi, Kandanchavadi, Chennai 600096

Westland and the Westland logo are the trademarks of Westland
Publications Private Limited, or its affi lates.

Copyright © Ravi Subramanian, 2020

ISBN: 9789388689519

This is a work of fi ction. Names, characters, organisations, places,
events and incidents are either products of the authors' imagination
or used fi ctiously.

Typeset by R. Ajith Kumar

NOTE ON SHORTZ

For my readers who love pace, I present *Shortz* – Thrills Uninterrupted. I've conceptualised these books as a series of short, plot-oriented, fast paced novellas that are the book equivalent of caffeine for an exhausted mind. These are thrillers on steroids. There isn't a slow moment in these books, not a sentence that does not take the story forward, not a page that doesn't beg to be turned. Airports, railway stations, flights, buses, metros, bedrooms or even behind your laptops—you'd want to read your own copy of *Shortz* everywhere. These stories promise to hold you firmly in their grip until you reach the very end.

Shortz serves another purpose. I noticed that in our country, mythology and romance are popular genres and draw many capable writers. Crime writing though is often considered too complicated, and has not seen many writers emerge. My co-authors in *Shortz* are all brilliant writers, hand-picked by me to fill this gap. Each thriller in this series is written by a talented author with a definite flair for crime writing. It has been a pleasure to work with them and to be able to provide a platform for them.

With short, fast paced, pulse pounding, high impact, no flab stories, *Shortz* comes with a built in accelerator. So fasten your seatbelts and get ready for the ride!

Ravi Subramanian

ONE

Meera Dixit, Assistant Superintendent of Police, turned right at the Metro Cinema junction towards Chhatrapati Shivaji Terminus. CST, as it is popularly called, is a historic railway station and a World Heritage site in Mumbai. It was 1 a.m. on a cold Sunday in December, but the city was still wide awake. After a relatively easy day at work, Meera was in a good mood. *Easy day, so far*, she hastily reminded herself.

She had spent the day at the Brabourne Stadium. Meera was overseeing police security arrangements for an American pop star's concert, which was scheduled for the following week. She was surprised, and just a little bit amused, to see a huge crowd, mostly teenagers, already queueing up to buy tickets. Most of them would have to go back empty-handed, she guessed. The minimum ticket price was five thousand rupees—wasn't *that* criminal?

Meera had grown up in Pune, Mumbai's more sedate satellite city. She often wondered when her hometown would catch up with the madness of the Maximum City, if ever.

She drove her police car, a white Bolero, through the gates of the Azad Maidan police station and parked it in the compound. She got off the vehicle, adjusted the peaked cap over her pretty, oval face in a habitual gesture and looked up at the structure. This 128-year-old stone edifice had been home for the past two years where she was serving as a station officer. She strode in, past the reception area and waiting room, into her spacious open office. The constable on duty stood up to salute Meera; she acknowledged him and sat down, picking up the file on top of the stack on her desk.

'Salunkhe, anything important?' she asked the constable, without looking up.

'Nothing, madam,' he replied.

'That's good.' *Crime appears to have gone on a vacation*, Meera thought.

Just then, a young canteen boy came in and placed a small glass of tea on Meera's desk. She gave him a dimpled smile, shut the file and took a sip of the strong chai. Her eyes followed the boy to the small twenty-four-hour cafeteria right next to the police station's entrance. It was still crowded with cops, even in the small hours. She sighed and got up.

'I am going home, Salunkhe. See you tomorrow. Goodnight.'

'Goodnight, madam.'

Meera was just about to step out of her office when the phone rang.

TWO

'Hello, Azad Maidan Police Station,' she said, picking up on the third ring. There was deafeningly loud music playing on the other end; she could hear nothing else.

'Hello, is anyone there?' asked Meera. There was no reply. She looked at Salunkhe and shrugged. He, too, stepped closer to the phone. Meera was holding the receiver a couple of inches away from her ear, but the sound was still ear-splitting. She was about to disconnect the call when the volume of the music abruptly decreased.

'Hello,' she repeated, slowly bringing the receiver closer to her ear.

'Please ... please, help me,' a weak voice said. Meera gestured to Salunkhe for a paper and pen, which he promptly produced.

'Who are you, sir? And where are you calling from?' Meera asked.

The line went dead.

'Who was it, madam?'

'No idea. He disconnected the phone. Maybe he'll call back.' Meera sat down at her desk again.

'I don't think …' ventured Salunkhe, but he was interrupted by the shrill ringing of the phone. Meera picked up immediately. 'Hello.'

'*Paradise* … Carter Road … Bandra. Please help me,' said the frightened voice on the other end of the line.

'But what is the problem?' asked Meera.

'My wife … she is trying to kill me.'

THREE

'Salunkhe, let's go,' said Meera, as she rushed out of the station, the constable close on her heels. Salunkhe took the Bolero's wheel and they sped out of the compound, heading north towards Bandra, popularly known as the Queen of the Suburbs, an upscale residential area in Mumbai. Carter Road, home to many Bollywood stars and wealthy industrialists, is a posh, sea-facing street in Bandra.

The streets were almost deserted; nevertheless, Salunkhe used the police siren to navigate through the light traffic. Meera was restless, thumping her fist on the dashboard in a slow, continuous rhythm, willing the car to go even faster than the steady ninety Salunkhe maintained.

'Do you know the address?' she asked Salunkhe.

'Yes, madam. It was on my beat a few years ago, when I was posted in the western suburbs,' he replied.

'Good.' Meera sighed.

It was exactly 1.40 a.m. when the car drew up near the address on Carter Road. Salunkhe pointed to a two-storeyed house that stood ominously, in almost complete darkness and isolation, at the dead end of the road. *Paradise.*

Across the road, the Arabian Sea lashed at the rocky shore angrily, spraying the promenade with salt water. *Paradise* was surrounded by a rock wall, almost six feet in height; there was no provision for a security cabin, not even a chair for a guard. Meera opened the old, squeaking gate and stepped into the garden. Salunkhe followed her. An enormous, twisted tree, hostile and sinister in appearance, stood at the centre of a large grassplot. Tall, unkempt grass had crept up everywhere.

A gravel driveway led up to the entrance of the house. It branched into two near the door, the entrance to its right and the wall to its left a little ahead. Meera sprinted lightly up the path to the main door. All the lights were switched off; there was no evidence of the loud music that had drowned out the man's voice on the call. She looked at Salunkhe, her raised eyebrows checking if they were at the right address. Salunkhe nodded and gestured towards the doorbell.

Meera pulled out her service revolver, murmured a silent prayer and rang the doorbell.

FOUR

The Headquarters of the Mumbai Police are situated in a gothic-style heritage building, directly opposite Crawford Market in south Mumbai. Made conspicuous by the dozen or so police vehicles parked outside, the place pulsed with an energy that matched the city's own rhythm.

Monday mornings, when Commissioner of Police Hemant Gokhale held his weekly meeting with the top brass of the Crime Branch, were especially busy. A veteran with more than thirty years of distinguished service in the force, Gokhale was credited with bringing crime rates in Mumbai down to an all-time low. The purpose of the meeting was to get a first-hand weekly update on what was happening in the city, to gauge what could be done to ensure the safety of citizens.

It also guaranteed that nobody in the Mumbai police force took things easy—not on Gokhale's watch, in any case.

In addition to the Crime Branch team, there were five other attendees—'high-potential' cops, recruited over the last three years. Gokhale had hand-picked these young talents to groom them for bigger roles in the future. Meera Dixit, who had graduated at the top of her class from the National Police Academy, Hyderabad, three years ago, was among them. She had caught Gokhale's attention at a VIP function when she had denied preferential treatment to a politician's son.

Meera was the first to reach the stately meeting room on the second floor. She made her way towards one end of the large rectangular table. Just then, Rohini Singh, a batchmate of Meera's from the Academy, came in. They exchanged a warm hug and sat down next to each other. Gokhale, a stickler for time, walked in at the stroke of nine. The other members of the team followed him.

In his characteristically crisp style, Gokhale ticked off the items on the agenda, making notes intermittently. 'Any other matters we should take note of?' he asked at the end of the meeting.

'Sir, if I may?' Meera spoke.

'Go ahead, Meera.'

She described the phone call she had received the previous night. And waited for reactions.

'So, what action did you take, Meera?' asked Gokhale.

'Sir, I immediately went to the address mentioned by the caller. But there was nobody there. I knocked at the door, checked the windows, the back door—nothing. No answer. But I think ...'

'Strange ... but in all likelihood, it was a crank call,' Gokhale said, as he picked up his diary and rose to leave.

'But what if there is something to it?' Meera persisted.

'Meera, notwithstanding the fact that crime rates have fallen, do you know how overworked the Mumbai police are? Our people are working double-shifts on most days. And we get such calls every day. Drop it.'

'Please let me investigate this for some more time, sir. I promise it won't come in the way of my existing cases.'

'Meera, we absolutely can't afford to waste resources on a wild goose chase,' Gokhale said, with an air of finality.

'But how can we risk leaving a civilian to die, without a proper follow-up? That too, after what appears to have been a desperate call for help?' a baritone voice spoke up. It was the Superintendent of Police, Aditya Sachdev. 'What if the caller was telling the truth, sir?'

Gokhale took off his reading glasses and sighed.

'What if someone is actually in danger? Should we not help him?' Aditya repeated.

'Of course, but …'

'Let me assess the situation once. If I end up with nothing, we will drop the case at once,' Aditya said.

'Okay, Aditya, you've made your point. Check it out, but use your judgement and keep me posted,' Gokhale said, as he left the room.

'Sure, sir,' Aditya said, and signalled to Meera to follow him.

'Lucky you,' whispered Rohini, as she nudged Meera and winked at her.

FIVE

The Mumbai police operate in five regions—North, South, East, West and Central—further divided into twelve zones, with an additional port zone. At thirty-six, Aditya Sachdev was one of the youngest police officers to head a zone. He was in charge of Zone 9, which, coincidentally, included Bandra, the location from where the anonymous call was supposedly made.

Aditya had, over the past few years, built a reputation as a no-nonsense, upright police officer with a heart of gold. His most recent case was a high-profile murder that had shaken the entire nation. A well-known socialite had been arrested for murdering her daughter in cold blood. Against all preconceived notions of a mother's unconditional love for her child, Aditya had followed his gut, pursued the investigation, clinched evidence and made the arrest.

With his lean and muscular physique, chiselled face and thick moustache, Aditya was a hit with the women. Needless to say, his single status only made him a more attractive proposition for the opposite sex.

'Let's go,' Aditya said to Meera, and walked out of the meeting room. Meera rushed after him, walking fast to keep up with his long strides.

They climbed down two flights of stairs, Meera narrating her telephonic conversation with the anonymous caller once more at Aditya's behest. He led her to a Toyota Innova parked at the entrance of the compound.

'Let's hope we are in time,' he said, easing the car out from Headquarters onto the busy Mumbai roads.

SIX

Bandra was about eighteen kilometres away, a forty-five minute ride at that time of the day.

'I have heard so much about you, sir,' ventured Meera, after a few minutes of silence. Without waiting for Aditya's response, she continued, 'One of the youngest SPs in the police force, recently commended by the Prime Minister at the All-India Police Conference. I mean, you are a role model, sir.'

Aditya shook his head with a wry smile. *Help me, please!* Without warning, the scream echoed in his ears, like it did a million times a day. He managed to acknowledge her words with a slight nod and diverted the topic. 'No need to call me *sir*,' he said. *If only she knew*, he thought.

Meera veered the conversation to her current assignment as station officer at Azad Maidan, seeking professional tips from Aditya. She found the discussion very engaging; Aditya offered insightful advice on effectively navigating the complex police organisation.

When he stopped the car at a red light near Worli, half-way to their destination, a knock on the window interrupted the conversation. It was a boy in his early teens, selling magazines and newspapers at the traffic signal.

'Hello, sir,' the boy greeted Aditya excitedly.

'Hey, Amol. How are you?' Hope you have not discontinued school?' Aditya addressed the boy as he rolled down the window.

'No, sir, I haven't. Can you drop me at the next signal?'

'Hop in,' said Aditya, and unlocked the door for the boy, who scampered in.

The light turned green and the car sped on. Meera was amazed at the conversation taking place between Aditya and Amol. The two seemed to know each other for many years now. And it was certainly unusual for a street urchin to like a cop as much as this boy clearly liked the SP.

Aditya halted briefly at the next junction; the boy jumped out and waved his thanks.

They crossed the Bandra-Worli sea-link, an engineering marvel connecting the western and southern suburbs of Mumbai, and reached Carter Road. Aditya seemed to know exactly where he was going, Meera noticed. As if reading her thoughts, he smiled and said, 'This is my zone. I know it like the back of my hand.'

SEVEN

Aditya parked the car, and they walked at a brisk pace towards the house. If ever there was a misnomer, this was it, he thought. For *Paradise* looked nothing like it.

The first floor of the two-storeyed house, oddly, was smaller in size than the ground floor. The entire building was constructed of cold, grey stone, intensifying the atmosphere of gloom that enveloped it.

A big plot of land lay on the right of the house. It was bare except for the visible remnants of an earlier structure that had been demolished or abandoned midway. Beyond the plot lay an arid, jagged stretch of uninhabited land. The elegantly paved, tree-lined Carter Road promenade seemed to merge with this desolate landscape and vanish, giving way to a local fishing village. To the left of *Paradise* stood a small single-storeyed cottage, painted bright white and yellow.

As Aditya approached the house, he noticed a set of tyre marks along the driveway, and traced them to a black Honda SUV parked carelessly near the wall. The car would have to be reversed out of the house, he thought, given that the driveway was not wide enough for it to make a U-turn.

Aditya also spotted a beaten trail branching out from the driveway. He walked down the path; it led to a small gate in the wall at the back of the house. Standing on tiptoe and peeping over the wall, he saw another vacant plot, which seemed to be an extension of the abandoned construction site next door. Behind this plot was a service road running parallel to Carter Road.

'Aditya,' Meera, who was two steps behind him, called out.

'Yeah,' he said, turning around.

'I just saw someone … behind those curtains,' she said, pointing to a closed glass window on the first floor, directly above them.

Aditya looked up. There was nobody at the window now, but he had a feeling that someone was watching them. 'Let's go inside,' he said, and they walked back to the main entrance.

For some strange reason, his hand was drawn to his

gun, and he was relieved to find it sitting snugly in the holster. With an eerie sensation that he was about to enter a mausoleum, Aditya rang the bell.

EIGHT

The heavy wooden door was opened by a man of slight build, with wild hair and a salt-and-pepper stubble. He regarded them with sad, distrustful eyes. Aditya estimated him to be in his late thirties, although he looked a decade older.

Aditya and Meera flashed their badges.

'I got a call last night …' said Meera.

'Yes, that was me. Rohit Acharya,' he said.

'I came over last night, but nobody answered the door,' Meera said.

'I am sorry, I didn't hear the doorbell … I … thanks anyway. Come in, please,' Rohit said.

Aditya and Meera stepped into the spacious but sparsely furnished living room. Three large brown sofas had been placed at the centre, with a low, wooden table between them. A chandelier, swaying gently in the sea breeze, was suspended directly above the table.

A hard rock music channel was playing at a high volume on the seventy-five-inch television. Rohit turned the music off and sat down on one of the sofas, inviting Aditya and Meera to take their seats on the one next to his.

'May I use the restroom before we start?' asked Meera.

'Sure, it's right over there,' said Rohit, pointing towards a passage to his left, next to a wide staircase that led up to the first floor. Meera nodded and headed that way, glancing up the stairs before turning into the passage.

Aditya and Rohit sat in silence, waiting for Meera. Two worn-out Persian rugs carpeted most of the living-room floor. Beyond this area was a dining table, with a provision for eight chairs. Only six were placed around it. A closed door by the table led to another room, possibly the kitchen, Aditya guessed.

The impression that overwhelmed Aditya, as he looked around, was that the house had eroded away, old and uncared for. The paint was peeling off the walls, which were bare except for a large mirror and a chime clock. The shelves were empty and the curtains were worn-out.

Once Meera had returned and sat down next to Aditya, the two officers got down to business.

'So, how can we help you, Mr Acharya?' asked Aditya.

'Please call me Rohit ... now, where do I start?' He sighed and continued after a pause, 'Tanvi and I have been married for fourteen years. We first met at a business seminar. I was presenting a paper on financial markets, and she was the recipient of the 'Young Entrepreneur' award that year. She had, at the time, recently joined her father's pharmaceutical business—Bakshi Pharma. I'm sure you have heard of it.'

Rohit looked at Aditya and Meera, who nodded.

'We were very happy together, content in our own small world, until a year ago. My father-in-law, Dev Bakshi, died in a car accident. Tanvi could not handle the loss and slipped into depression. She lost all interest in the business, or rather, in life itself.'

Aditya and Meera exchanged a glance, waiting for Rohit to continue.

'Soon, she started to fly into fits of rage, in the office, at home ... for no reason at all. Around six months back, I woke up one night and saw that Tanvi was not in bed. My first thought was she may have gone to the restroom, but I checked and she hadn't. I got worried and looked for her in the other room, but she wasn't there either. Then I heard something … footsteps … someone walking in the courtyard. I could see from the window on the floor above that it was Tanvi. I rushed down and called out to her. She did not respond. Then she looked right through me. That was when I realised she was walking in her sleep.'

'Was that the first time she sleepwalked?' asked Aditya.

'Yes, as far as I can say,' replied Rohit.

'But, isn't sleepwalking a fairly common disorder?' Meera asked.

'It is. But sleepwalking with a knife is not,' Rohit said.

NINE

'I was scared,' Rohit continued. 'I followed her ... two steps behind, calling out to her. But she continued walking—a strange expression on her face, knife in hand. She walked up to the tree in the garden, and stopped. Then she turned, went back to our bedroom, put the knife under her pillow and fell asleep.'

'Did you talk to her about it later?' asked Meera.

'I did, the next morning. But she had no recollection of it.'

'And then?'

'I took her to our family doctor, who referred us to a psychiatrist. It took me a few days to convince her to visit the psychiatrist. She underwent therapy for about two months. When therapy did not work for Tanvi, medication was prescribed. I learnt to keep track of the medicines and their dosages, so that I could administer them myself, should the need arise. But nothing seemed to have an effect on Tanvi. In fact, her condition has only worsened.'

'Worsened how?' asked Meera.

'The sleepwalking episodes have become more frequent. Every other night, she walks about in our room, up and down the staircase, and at times, goes out of the house. And then, one night ...' Rohit paused for a moment, evidently struggling to articulate what he was about to say. 'She tried to attack me with the knife. That was the first in a series of attacks—all in her sleep, of course. She had no idea what she was doing. Then ... two days ago, after I had fallen asleep ... she ... she stabbed me with a pair of scissors.'

Rohit rolled up his t-shirt sleeve to reveal a fresh wound on his left shoulder, about three inches wide, the stitches still visible.

'Oh my God!' Meera gasped, walking up to him to take a closer look.

'Have you thought about arranging for ... better care?' asked Aditya, choosing his words carefully.

'You mean like a mental institution? She is my wife, for God's sake,' said Rohit.

'No offence meant. It's just that she probably needs that level of care and attention,' said Aditya. 'Now tell us, Mr Acharya, how can *we* help?'

'I didn't know what to do ... so I called the police. I don't want anything to happen to Tanvi, but I also fear for my life.'

Rohit's hopeless dilemma saddened Aditya. *Help me, please*, the scream rang in his head again, *I don't want to die.*

'We'll see how we can help,' he said finally, patting Rohit's back as he noted Tanvi's psychiatrist's details.

'Thank you very much,' said Rohit.

'And where is she now?' asked Meera.

'Upstairs. In her room.'

'Can we see her? Talk to her?'

'Not sure if talking will help. She may not even be awake. Anyway, come with me,' said Rohit, as he led them towards the staircase.

'One more thing,' said Meera, as they walked up the creaking stairs, 'what's with the constant loud music?'

'Ever since all this started, I've had difficulty sleeping. Since the attacks began, I have been, in fact, afraid of falling asleep. The loud music is to ensure I don't, just in case.'

TEN

There were two rooms on the first floor, one at each end of a long corridor. Rohit gently opened the door to the room on the right. Aditya and Meera exchanged an apprehensive glance before following their host into the room.

It resembled a hospital room. The colours were dull and the walls were painted light blue, except for the pale floral wallpaper on the one behind the large double bed. On it, a figure in a white hospital gown lay motionless. Tanvi Acharya was a tall, slim woman with long, brown hair. There was a glow on her face, despite the long bout of illness and depression she had experienced.

Rohit bent over the bed and kissed her forehead. Tanvi did not stir. 'She is fast asleep. Must be the medicines,' Rohit said.

Aditya walked to one of the windows looking out on the backyard. It was the same window Meera had pointed to earlier, when she thought someone was watching them. Then he looked again at the motionless figure of Tanvi Acharya.

'Let's not disturb her,' said Aditya.

They walked out of the room and down the stairs in silence.

'We'll be in touch,' Aditya told Rohit, who saw them to the door.

'Thanks for coming,' Rohit replied.

'Take down our numbers, in case of new developments,' Meera said to Rohit.

They exchanged numbers, Meera smiling to herself as she made a mental note of Aditya's number.

ELEVEN

Aditya and Meera walked back to the car and were about to drive off when she said, pointing to the white and yellow cottage next door, 'Why don't we speak to the neighbour? He may tell us something useful.'

'Good idea,' Aditya concurred.

They approached the house, which was, in many ways, a complete contrast to *Paradise*. It appeared newly painted and well-maintained. 'Mehta Mahal - 1942' was engraved on a pillar at the entrance. Pushing open the gate's iron grille, they saw a thin, silver-haired old man in dark-blue shorts and a yellow t-shirt. He was watering plants that neatly bordered a manicured lawn.

'Hi, how can I help you?' the old man waved and called out to them in a pleasant voice.

Aditya and Meera introduced themselves.

'Sam. Sam Mehta.' With a cheerful smile, he ushered them to the cane chairs on the patio.

'Nice house, Sam. You live alone?' asked Meera.

'Thanks. Yes, since my wife passed away three years ago, I live alone.' He sighed, removing his gold-rimmed glasses. 'My children are in America. I lived there too, for many years, before I retired and moved back here.'

'Actually, Sam, we are here to talk to you about your neighbours—Rohit and Tanvi Acharya,' said Aditya. 'We just met Rohit.'

'Why? Has something happened?' Sam asked, a hint of worry in his voice.

'No, just routine questioning,' said Meera and briefly explained why they had paid a visit to *Paradise*.

'Yeah, I feel very sad for them. They were such a happy couple when I first met them. But then, Dev died and … you know about Tanvi. Poor girl!'

'Have you noticed anything unusual about her?'

'I used to go over sometimes. But not anymore. Over the past months, I've seen her condition deteriorate steadily—sleepwalking and all that.'

'Have you ever seen her walking in her sleep?' asked Meera.

'Yes, I did, once. About a month ago, walking in her

courtyard at night. I believe she is mostly in bed these days, and rightly so.'

'Why do you say that?' asked Meera.

'Oh, I'm sure you heard that she stabbed Rohit in her sleep. Poor man! He was sobbing when he told me about it yesterday. I hope things work out for the best.'

'We hope so, too,' said Meera, as she and Aditya got up to leave.

'Thank you for your time, Sam. This is my contact number. If you see anything unusual or worrisome, please call me,' Aditya said, giving his details to Sam.

'Sure, I will.'

TWELVE

'I am intrigued,' said Meera, as they drove to Bandra Police Station, where Aditya operated from on most days.

'About what?'

'First, such a huge house and no domestic help. I didn't see a single maid, cook or security guard. I will ask Rohit about that tomorrow.' She made a note in a small, black diary.

'Good point.' Aditya nodded his approval.

'Secondly, if Rohit is so scared of being attacked, why doesn't he keep the knives, scissors and other sharp objects hidden?'

'Yes, I thought of that too.'

'And?'

'You know, Meera, when someone really wants to harm you, a weapon is not needed. How many things can Rohit hide? Tanvi seems like a strong woman, and her husband has a frail physique. She could strangle him, push him down the stairs or bang his head against the wall … you get the point?'

'Hmm … he must be terrified … no wonder he is unable to sleep. I feel sorry for him. Aditya, is there a way we can help him?'

'Well, we should,' said Aditya. *I don't want to die! Aditya shivered as he stepped out of the door, the cold wind sending shivers down his spine. Wait, don't do that, he screamed.* Pushing the lid down on the memory, he continued, 'It seems he has no one else to turn to; that's why he called us. Also, being in the thick of things, he evidently cannot think clearly. So we have to see how best to equip him to help himself; or maybe there's another way that we haven't figured out yet.'

Meera nodded in agreement. It was 4 p.m. when they reached Bandra Police Station. As they walked in, the respect that Aditya commanded from his team was palpable in the demeanour of his subordinates. Once they were seated in his cabin, Aditya said, 'I am famished; let's have lunch.'

Meera finished her lunch quickly and stepped out of the cabin for a few minutes. When she returned, Aditya was still eating.

'I just spoke to Rohit to ask him about the domestic help situation,' said Meera. 'He said there's a maid who comes in daily to clean up. He manages the cooking himself; he likes to cook, he says, and it keeps him occupied. As for a security guard, he said he doesn't need one as there's nothing valuable in the house.'

She took her diary out and struck off the item from her 'to-do' list. Aditya smiled.

'So, what do you think we should do next?' asked Aditya, curious to know how her mind worked while on a case.

'Visit Tanvi's psychiatrist and the Bakshi Pharma office,' she said promptly.

'Good. I will pick you up tomorrow. Where do you live?'

'Parel Police Colony.'

'9 a.m. sharp.'

Meera smiled and took her leave. Aditya saw her out to a patrol car. He was impressed by the investigative acumen she had displayed. She would rise to the top one day, he thought. *She is also very pretty*, he could not help thinking.

THIRTEEN

The head office of Bakshi Pharma was a state-of-the-art, seven-storeyed building in Bandra-Kurla Complex, popularly known as BKC. Over the last decade, BKC had replaced the south Mumbai area of Nariman Point as the commercial hub of the city.

Aditya and Meera were seated in the opulent reception area, waiting for Pratap Chauhan, the executive director of the company as well as acting CEO in Tanvi's absence. Aditya was thumbing through the pages of the latest issue of *Business Today*. The cover story was on Bakshi Pharma, and featured an interview with Pratap Chauhan. The article also had a file photo of a beaming Dev Bakshi, with his beautiful daughter, Tanvi. 'In safe hands', read the caption below the photograph.

Aditya pointed out to a sub-heading in the article: 'Bakshi Pharma valued at rupees 2,000 crores'. Meera let out a soft whistle.

'What else did Rohit tell you about Pratap Chauhan?' Aditya asked. He had instructed Meera to speak with Rohit to get some background on the company, which she had done that morning.

'He said that Pratap Chauhan started his career with the company, and was Dev Bakshi's most trusted aide,' Meera replied. 'Chauhan has been like a father-figure to Tanvi after Bakshi passed away and has been running the company since she became unwell.'

Just then, a young woman in a business suit came up to them. 'Mr Sachdev and Ms Dixit, Mr Chauhan will see you now. Please follow me.'

FOURTEEN

She led them across the vast and tastefully decorated reception area to a large corner office. Aditya noticed that a similar cabin on the opposite side had been reserved for Tanvi. Chauhan's office resembled a five-star suite, with its plush leather upholstery, teakwood furniture and French windows. It offered a magnificent view of the lush green field of the MCA club.

Pratap Chauhan was a tall, lean man, almost completely bald, with warm eyes and an equally warm smile. He looked exceptionally fit for a man of his age. He led them to a separate seating area in the office.

Introductions done, Chauhan got down to business. 'So, Inspector Sachdev, how may I help you?'

'We wanted to ask you about Tanvi Acharya and your impressions of her state of mind over the past months,' Aditya said.

'I have known Tanvi for many years now. She is an independent and intelligent young woman. Even I had not imagined that Dev's death would have such a devastating impact on her. She just ... became a very different person after he died. Depressed and angry all the time. Lost interest in the business; almost stopped coming to work. And when she did, she would behave very strangely.'

'Angry, you say? Angry about what?'

'Well, Dev, Tanvi's father, died in a car accident on the Mumbai-Pune highway. A speeding truck hit his car, and it plunged off a cliff. Even his body could not be recovered. Actually, Tanvi was supposed to join him on that trip, but she changed her mind at the last minute. She believes she could somehow have saved him, had she accompanied him on that fatal journey.'

'You also say she behaved strangely when she came to work after Mr Bakshi's demise. Could you please elaborate?' Meera asked.

'Earlier, Tanvi was a polite, courteous person. And very rational in her decisions. After this incident, she would often get angry at everyone—at times, for no reason at all. She would take business decisions that made no sense, sack people at the drop of a hat. There was every possibility that the company's performance would be affected by her erratic behaviour. That is when the Board decided that I should take over as Acting CEO until she recovers completely and is fit to resume her duties.'

'And when do you think that is likely to happen?' asked Meera.

'While I hope she recovers as soon as possible, I understand that her condition is not getting any better. I heard she attacked Rohit ...?' Chauhan asked, looking at Aditya and Meera for confirmation.

'She is unwell, that's true. But we are unable to comment on her medical condition,' replied Meera. *Good answer*, Aditya thought, observing her with a quiet smile.

'How well do you know Rohit?' Aditya asked Chauhan.

'Personally, not too well; I have met him socially a few times, that's all. Of course, he is a stakeholder in the company, so he does attend board meetings once in a while.'

'So he was never closely involved in the business?'

'Not really, which is a bit surprising, considering that he, too, has a background in finance. But he was never the ambitious sort. I believe him to be a kind human being who wants to change society for the better. I think he has been associated with an NGO for the past five years or so, although these days, I think, he spends all his time at home, taking care of Tanvi.'

FIFTEEN

Aditya eased his Innova onto the Western Express Highway, which had relatively light traffic even in peak office hours. *Thank the holiday season*, he thought. The sun was overhead, but a cold breeze freshened the air. Meera, too, seemed to be enjoying the weather, as she had rolled down the window.

Aditya remarked, 'The weather in Mumbai has been enjoyable these past few winters.'

'Since the time I moved here, I guess,' Meera said.

'So, that's the reason!' said Aditya, and they both laughed.

As they neared the Bandra East junction, Aditya pointed to a residential complex on his right. 'This is where I stay—Bandra Police Colony.'

'Where is your family, Aditya?'

'In Mumbai, I live alone. My parents are in Lucknow, with my brother and his family. How about you?'

'I, too, live alone here. I have a small flat in Pune, which I maintain and visit from time to time ... I grew up there. My parents are in our village near Kolhapur.'

'And, are you still single? Sorry, you don't have to answer that,' Aditya said, immediately regretting the fact that he had ventured a personal question so soon.

'That's okay. Yes, I am indeed single.' Meera smiled and continued, 'And I will not ask you the same question. Because I know you are.'

'How do you know that?' asked Aditya, surprised.

Meera merely smiled in response. 'Shall we grab a quick bite before we meet the doctor?' she asked.

SIXTEEN

Aditya and Meera reached Dr Binaaz Mistry's clinic, located in the peaceful Five Gardens area of Dadar Parsi Colony in central Mumbai. As the name suggests, this section of the colony has a cluster of five gardens, interconnected by a circular avenue lined with trees. The gardens were laid out in the early nineteenth century by a prominent Parsi family of the time.

Dr Mistry's clinic was on the ground floor of a recently constructed, towering sixteen-storeyed structure. It looked slightly out of place among its more old-fashioned neighbours, most of them no higher than two storeys.

'Please wait, Dr Mistry is with a patient,' the receptionist informed them, and bade them to sit in the comfortable waiting area. It was another twenty minutes before the door to the consultation room opened. A young woman walked out, audibly thanking the doctor.

'You may go in now,' the receptionist told Aditya and Meera.

Dr Mistry, an amiable lady in her early forties, was seated at her desk, dressed in elegant formals. She invited them warmly to sit in comfortable leather chairs opposite hers. The clinic was aesthetically designed, with warm-hued walls and soft carpeting. Aditya noticed the framed certificate on the wall: 'Gold Medalist, M.D., All India Institute of Medical Sciences, 1999'.

When he had called to fix the appointment, Aditya had explained the reason for their visit to Dr Mistry. The psychiatrist had kept Tanvi's case file handy, which she now placed on the table.

'We hope to gain a better understanding of Tanvi Acharya's case, Dr Mistry,' Aditya began.

'Tanvi's case was referred to me by the Acharyas' family doctor around six months ago. When she was brought to me, she was bordering on paranoid schizophrenia, presumably triggered, in her case, by the trauma of losing her father in an accident. Her sleepwalking episodes are also a result of this psychiatric disorder,' Dr Mistry said. 'Needless to say, I performed a range of laboratory as well as psychological tests on her before finalising my diagnosis.'

'Is it fairly common for people who sleepwalk to not remember having done so?' Meera asked.

'It is the norm, Meera. Almost all people who sleepwalk have no memory of their episodes at all,' Dr Mistry smiled.

'And can they harm other people in that state?'

'It is entirely possible, as in Tanvi's case, although such incidents are rare.'

'What is the cure for such cases then?'

'It takes time, sometimes years; often, the patient is never fully cured. In Tanvi's case, I started with psychotherapy sessions. When she did not respond favourably, I put her on medication—mild antidepressants and sleeping pills. In the event of an extreme emergency, I had prescribed a sedative injection.'

'And how would you rate her progress thus far?' Aditya asked.

'I have to admit that her condition is not improving. I have consulted a few of my colleagues on this case, and I am doing the best I can. However, it seems that the wisest course of action, which I have already recommended to Rohit, is to admit her to an institution.

But he is not willing to do that. He thinks Tanvi will be best taken care of at home.'

'Actually, our concern is more for Rohit,' Aditya said.

'Yes, mine too. His insomnia is partly a disorder, but mostly fear. I suggested sleep-inducing hypnotics to him, but he refused. Too scared to sleep, he says,' Dr Mistry added.

SEVENTEEN

'So, how is the investigation progressing on Meera's case? The one you are helping with?' Gokhale asked Aditya. A month had passed since Rohit's phone call to the Azad Maidan Police Station.

They were returning from a meeting with the Chief Minister. Gokhale had just presented an ambitious proposal to the minister to enhance the dynamic capacity of the severely short-staffed Mumbai police force. The idea was to employ temporary personnel in the police force when demands on their capacity were higher, during events such as festivals and VIP visits, and in emergency situations such as terrorist attacks. The plan also reduced the strain on their already restricted budgets. The minister had a favourable first impression of the proposal and promised Gokhale to give it a serious push in the State Assembly.

'It is a complicated case, sir. On the one hand, we don't have reasonable grounds for the arrest of Tanvi Acharya. On the other, we cannot guarantee the safety of Rohit Acharya. We'll simply have to wait and intervene at the right time. Meera and I met the police psychiatrist to hear his views on the case. We also did a fair bit of research among our archives to see if there have been similar cases in the past,' said Aditya.

'And?'

'This is a unique case, sir. We have to tread very carefully.'

'I hope ... you're not getting so involved in the case because of what happened, right?' Gokhale looked at Aditya, concerned.

Aditya stared out of the window in pensive silence for a moment or two before he replied, 'No, sir. It is not that.'

'It was not your fault, Aditya.'

EIGHTEEN

It was 11 a.m. when Aditya dropped Gokhale at the Police Headquarters. He then drove to Azad Maidan Police Station, which was less than a kilometre away.

Over the past month, he and Meera had spent a lot of time together on the case. He found, rather to his surprise, that he was strongly attracted to her. He had never felt this way about anyone since a crushing heartbreak eight years ago. But Meera was different from any other woman he had met—smart, beautiful, and singularly committed to her work. Above all, being a policewoman herself, she seemed to understand Aditya through and through, from his investigative instincts to his erratic lifestyle. *Let's see where this takes us*, he thought.

He walked into Meera's office and found that she was in a meeting with her team. She smiled and waved at Aditya, who indicated he would wait for her outside.

'Good morning, Aditya,' she said, as she walked up to him ten minutes later.

'Chai?' he proposed, and they went into the cafeteria.

'So, how was the presentation? What did the Chief Minister say?'

'Gokhale sir is optimistic; me, not so much.'

'Stop being cynical,' she laughed.

Just then, a constable came running into the cafeteria. 'Madam, there is an emergency!'

NINETEEN

Police siren blaring, Meera sped her Bolero towards the World Trade Centre, situated on the southern tip of Mumbai. Aditya was in the passenger seat, scanning live updates on his phone. They reached the WTC in less than seven minutes.

The area outside the building was cordoned off. Two police patrol cars and four vans belonging to leading news channels were already parked on the road outside. Reporters were speaking and gesturing in front of cameras, with the WTC in the background, reporting live as the story broke. A large crowd had gathered, and the police were having a tough time controlling it.

'Where is he?' Aditya asked a policeman, who saluted him.

'He is on the first level, sir. Just above the escalator. He's holding a woman hostage, has a gun pointed at her head. Sub-Inspector Apte is at the entrance.'

Aditya and Meera ran to the entrance.

'What does he want?' Aditya asked Apte.

'Hasn't specified. He is just threatening to kill her and anyone else who tries to stop him. Seems to be a nutcase,' Apte said.

'How many other civilians inside?'

'There are around twenty shops and offices on the ground and first levels. Including the staff and customers, somewhere between 120 to 130 people, I guess.'

'Go to the WTC administration. Make an announcement on the PA system, asking everyone to get into the nearest shop and stay inside until they hear from us.'

'Yes, sir.'

'Meera, come with me,' Aditya said, and they went in.

TWENTY

Aditya and Meera went through the revolving doors and entered the huge, circular, black-and-white-tiled lobby of the WTC. After a minute, the PA system blared the announcement Aditya had asked for. Most of the people inside the building had already taken refuge in the shops; the remaining stragglers rushed into the nearest ones on hearing the broadcast. Curious and terrified heads popped up behind the glass windows of shops all around, like spectators in a macabre amphitheatre, waiting, perversely, to witness all the action.

Aditya saw the gunman on the first level, at the centre of the lobby. The neck of a terrified young woman was locked in the crook of his left arm. He was holding a small country-made revolver in his right hand, looking furiously in all directions, and muttering in the woman's ear from time to time.

'This is Inspector Aditya. I'm coming up to talk to you,' shouted Aditya, from the ground level. 'Everything will be all right; don't do anything stupid.'

'Don't come near me or I will shoot her,' the man shouted, and his captive screamed.

'I just want to talk,' Aditya said, as he stepped on the escalator, his hands raised above his head, revolver tucked in the back of his trousers. Meera followed him, crouching two steps below Aditya on the escalator as it slowly moved up towards the gunman and his hostage. Reaching the first level, they warily took positions on either side of the gunman, hands still above their heads.

'What do you want?' asked Aditya.

'Who is she?' the gunman asked, pointing towards Meera.

'She is with me. We just want to talk and see how we can resolve this. First, let the lady go.'

The gunman did not reply. He looked at Aditya, then at Meera, muttered inaudibly and pressed the gun harder into his captive's temple.

Aditya looked at Meera and gave her a slight nod. Taking cue, Meera said, 'Let her go. You can take me as a hostage instead.' And she took a single step towards the gunman.

'Stay where you are,' the gunman shouted, his attention now focused on Meera.

It was only a moment's diversion, but Aditya took advantage of it to draw out his gun. Aiming it at the gunman's forehead, he said, 'Drop your gun, or I will shoot you.'

The gunman looked confused now, as if unable to make up his mind about what to do next. His finger increased its pressure on the trigger. 'Stay away or ...' The sentence was cut short by the powerful sound of a gunshot.

The hostage screamed. Meera looked at Aditya and then at his smoking gun. The gunman dropped his gun as he fell, slumping forward. Aditya kicked the gun away. Meera gathered her wits and took the hysterical young woman down the escalator.

Apte came running up, followed by other policemen, all with their guns drawn out.

'Take him to the hospital. He should be fine in a week,' Aditya told Apte, pointing at the grimacing gunman, who was holding his right thigh where the bullet had hit him.

Aditya walked out of WTC, checking his phone. There was chaos outside the building; the media had gone into overdrive. Meera came running to him.

'Is she okay?' Aditya asked, referring to the hostage.

'She will be fine. Just shocked at the moment.'

'That's good.'

'Why did you shoot him?'

'What option did I have? He would have killed the woman,' Aditya said.

'But you didn't know that.'

'One can never know for sure, but an innocent life was at stake – why take a chance?'

TWENTY-ONE

The next morning, Aditya woke up earlier than his usual 5 a.m. and went for a swim. The pool was empty, the water glowing eerily in the dim lights. Aditya stood on the tiled edge for a moment and then dived in. The water was icy cold; he felt the blood freezing in his veins. He swam furiously to let the shock wear off. After half a lap, he felt in control of his muscles again and eased into his rhythm.

As he turned for his second lap, he heard the scream. It seemed to be coming from the depths of the pool.

Help me, please! I don't want to die!

Aditya tried to scream back and shut the voice up inside his head. But he couldn't.

He heard the siren of his patrol car. And footsteps. His own. As he ran towards the building.

It was eleven in the night. Four years ago. Aditya ran past the crowd that had gathered on the street and took the elevator to the nineteenth floor. A few people were in the hallway, standing about in their nightwear. A middle-aged couple was trying to break open a grille that obstructed them from taking the staircase to the terrace. They were shaking it violently, weeping and shouting incoherently.

'Please save my daughter,' the man implored Aditya. 'He says he loves her … then why is he doing this …'

'Step back,' Aditya said as he took out his revolver and fired a shot at the lock, snapping it open. 'Wait here,' he yelled as he slid open the grille and ran up the twelve steps to the terrace door. As he opened the door and stared into the darkness outside, a cold, harsh wind hit him, chilling him to the bone.

He saw the two intertwined figures at the far end of the terrace, as if suspended in the air. He put his gun down on the concrete floor and slowly walked towards them. The girl, no more than twenty, was sobbing softly. A young man, about her age, had an arm around her waist and a hand around her neck, gripping her tightly. They were standing on a ledge, a foot wide, that went around the terrace. Aditya looked down over the ledge at the street and felt dizzy.

'Let's talk. Everything will be all right,' Aditya said, raising both his hands.

'No ... it won't,' the man said.

'I promise you ... just step down. You love her, don't you?' Aditya stepped forward, hands still raised, eyes making contact with the man's.

'But she doesn't ...'

'Help me, please. I don't want to die,' the girl cried, looking at Aditya.

'Nobody can help us now,' the man said and took half a step backwards, one of his heels now an inch outside the ledge, his grip on the girl still firm.

'Wait ... don't do that!' Aditya shouted and rushed forward, arms outstretched. The man took one final step back and fell, taking the screaming girl with him into the void.

Aditya made a desperate attempt to clutch at something, anything, but he saw the two bodies plunge, making short work of the long way down. He turned his head away before they hit the ground. He heard the muted thuds though.

TWENTY-TWO

Unable to continue his swim, Aditya returned home from the pool earlier than usual. Despite professional help, and his best efforts to pretend that he was not affected by the incident, it continued to haunt him. Gokhale had been a pillar of strength, standing by and assuring him that he had done his best, and that neither he nor anyone else in his position could have changed the outcome.

He picked up the newspaper as he unlocked his door. 'Shootout at World Trade Centre', screamed the headlines on the front page. Another article on the second page was headlined 'Hero Cop saves Woman Hostage', while the National Human Rights Commission condemned the shooting as 'yet another police atrocity.' Aditya scanned the newspaper for ten minutes and then went to take a shower.

He was fixing himself breakfast when his phone beeped. It was a message from Gokhale. *Well done.* He had just sat down at the breakfast table, allowing himself a slight smile, when his phone rang again. It was Meera.

'Aditya, Rohit called. We need to go. Pick you up in thirty minutes?'

Aditya sighed. 'Okay,' he said.

'I … I am sorry you got involved in this case, Aditya.'

'No need to apologise. I am doing this for myself,' Aditya replied.

TWENTY-THREE

Meera parked the car right outside *Paradise*. They closed the iron grille behind them and hurried towards the entrance. Suddenly, Meera tugged at Aditya's shirt. He followed her gaze to the window on the first floor. For a moment, he thought he had seen a ghost—a woman with long, dishevelled hair, in a white gown, was staring down at them. Her palms were pressing hard against the windowpane, as if wanting to push it out of its frame.

Aditya and Meera stood frozen in the garden, unable to take their eyes off Tanvi. And then she was gone, drawing the curtains abruptly. Aditya felt she was still standing behind them, watching. He noticed that Meera was clinging to him. He put an arm around her.

'Are you okay?' he asked.

'I am fine,' she exhaled.

Aditya rang the bell.

Rohit's condition seemed to have worsened considerably since they had last seen him. He appeared to have aged several years over the past month; his eyes had sunk even deeper in their sockets. Music blared inside the house. Aditya recognised the song that was playing as a Scorpions classic, something he might have enjoyed listening to under different circumstances. Rohit picked up the remote and switched the television off.

'Another episode?' Aditya asked.

Rohit nodded weakly and poured himself a refill of black coffee from a large thermos on the living room table. 'Help yourselves,' he told Aditya and Meera, as they sat down on the sofa next to his.

Ignoring the courtesy, Aditya said, 'We've spoken to some experts, Rohit. There may or may not be a cure for Tanvi's condition. Why don't you reconsider …?'

'Out of the question,' Rohit interrupted, with a finality that implied he did not want to discuss the point any further.

Aditya sighed. He was about to say something when they heard a creaking sound on the wooden stairs. Meera jumped, and looked at Aditya. Slowly, as if in a trance, Tanvi came down the staircase and walked into the living room.

Meera shifted closer to Aditya. Rohit simply stared at Tanvi, mouth agape and eyes fraught with fear. Tanvi looked at each of them, one by one, without expression. Then she sat down on the third sofa.

Complete silence ensued. Nobody moved, or spoke. Tanvi stared into empty space for several minutes. Suddenly, she lunged for the thermos on the table and flung it at Rohit. He tried to duck, but it caught him on his shoulder, making him grimace in pain. Aditya sprang into action and waylaid Tanvi as she advanced towards Rohit.

'Hold her. I will get her medicine,' Rohit panted, as he ran up the staircase. Tanvi was screaming now, but Aditya had a firm grip on her and eventually managed to make her sit on the sofa. Meera moved closer to Aditya, trying to assist him.

Rohit came down, carrying a disposable syringe filled with a transparent drug. While Aditya held Tanvi, Rohit removed the cap off the syringe. Aditya noticed countless tiny spots on Tanvi's right forearm before Rohit jabbed the syringe right amidst them, creating one more. Tanvi's screams subsided, and within seconds, she had collapsed on the sofa.

TWENTY-FOUR

'What are you thinking?' Meera asked Aditya, who had not spoken a word since they left *Paradise*.

'Umm … I noticed something that is bothering me,' Aditya replied. 'Do you remember what Dr Mistry had said? About Tanvi's treatment?'

Meera looked at him inquiringly.

'She had prescribed an injection only in *extreme emergencies*. But, when I saw Tanvi's arm today, I saw so many marks …' His voice trailed off.

'Yeah, now that you mention it, I noticed that too. But …'

'But what?' Aditya asked.

'We've already seen how violent Tanvi can be. She has stabbed him once. And today, she attacked him again. How else is Rohit supposed to control her and save himself? He faces this day in and day out.'

'I guess you are right. I wish he would agree to move her to an institution.'

'He loves her, Aditya. He won't let go.'

TWENTY-FIVE

Aditya realised the case had shaken Meera and that beneath her tough exterior, there was a tender, caring core. *Maybe she's not as tough as she thinks she is*, he thought. He found her even more attractive in her vulnerability. It drew him closer to her, made him want to protect her. *You have fallen in love*, he told himself.

He picked up the phone and dialled Meera's number. It was 9 p.m. She answered at the first ring.

'Hi, how are you doing?' he asked.

'Okay, just a little stressed, I think.'

'That's police life for you. You will get used to it.'

'I am not sure if I want to get used to it, Aditya.'

Both of them did not speak for a few seconds.

'Do you want to go for a drive?' Aditya asked.

Aditya and Meera were out until 1 a.m. that night. They ate kebabs and rolls at Bademiya, one of

Mumbai's most famous eateries. They walked under moonlit skies at the Gateway of India, talking and laughing. Meera was fascinated with Aditya's childhood tales—about growing up in Lucknow; the decision to pursue a career in the police force despite an assured place in the family business; and his little niece, whom he seemed to absolutely adore. Aditya found himself opening up to Meera like he had with no one else.

Meera told him about her difficult childhood in her native village in Kolhapur, and the bias independent-minded women faced in such communities that prompted her to move to Pune, alone, at the vulnerable age of sixteen.

'You are not alone anymore,' Aditya said and hugged her. Holding her close, he discovered a comfort in her warm embrace, a sensation he had never experienced before. He did not want to let go. Ever.

'I love you, Aditya,' Meera said, gazing into his eyes.

'I love you too,' Aditya said.

TWENTY-SIX

It was 6 a.m. the next morning when Aditya's phone buzzed on his bedside table. He reached out for it and saw that it was Rohit calling. Meera was still asleep next to him. Not wanting to disturb her, he stepped out of the bedroom onto the balcony.

'Hello, Rohit. What's wrong?'

'Tanvi. She is missing. Can you come here immediately?'

Aditya was in two minds whether to rouse Meera or not. Finally, he gently nudged her awake. 'Hey, we need to go,' he said.

They were on the road within ten minutes. The streets were relatively free of traffic at that early hour, but not completely deserted. *The city never sleeps*, Aditya thought, as they sped towards *Paradise*. He drove the car into the compound and parked it near the main entrance of the house. The Honda was nowhere to be seen, and Aditya wondered if Rohit was at home.

However, he opened the door before they could ring the bell.

'What's up? Where is Tanvi?' Aditya asked him as they stepped inside.

'This morning, at around five-thirty, I realised she was missing. I looked everywhere in the house but could not find her. That's when I saw that the car is missing. And I called you. She must have driven off somewhere—I am so worried, Aditya,' Rohit said, pacing nervously across the room.

'Is she capable of driving a car in her current state?' asked Meera.

'Must be. I mean, she has not been driving these last months, but ...'

Aditya called a contact in the Road Transport Department. He gave him the details of the car and Tanvi's description. 'Please alert me as soon as you hear something,' he told the contact.

'It's all my fault,' said Rohit, agonised.

'It's not. Don't worry, we will find her,' Aditya reassured him.

An hour had passed before Rohit's phone rang. 'Hello,' he answered at the first ring. 'What? Okay, I will be right there.'

'Pratap Chauhan called. Tanvi is at the office,' he said, and they all rushed out.

They drove in Aditya's car to Bakshi Pharma's office in BKC. As they approached the building, Rohit exclaimed, 'There it is, our car!' The Honda was parked near the main entrance, its front wheels on the sidewalk, its bonnet mere inches from a lamppost.

It was not yet 8 a.m., and the building was more or less empty. The cleaners were at work when they reached the office floor. Pratap Chauhan, always among the early birds, was standing outside his cabin, looking nervous.

'Thank God you have come,' he said.

'Is she in there?' Rohit asked, moving towards Tanvi's cabin.

'Not there. Here,' said Chauhan, opening the door to his own office. Aditya followed Rohit in, Meera and Chauhan behind them. Tanvi was sitting at Chauhan's desk. Dressed in her hospital gown, her long hair unkempt, she was playing with the glass paperweight, humming a tune they could not recognise.

'Hello, Pratap uncle. Where is Papa? Didn't he come with you?' she asked Chauhan.

'Tanvi,' Rohit began.

'Who are you?' she asked him.

'You don't recognise me? I am Rohit ... your husband.'

Tanvi did not respond. She began to fiddle with the paperweight again. Aditya moved closer to Meera.

A few employees had gathered outside the cabin, curious to know what was going on. They had heard Tanvi was not well, but seeing her in this condition clearly surprised them. Chauhan asked one of them to call security. He promptly obeyed.

'Tanvi ...' Rohit ventured again, taking a step forward.

'Get out!' Tanvi screamed and hurled the paperweight at Rohit. It missed him by inches, smashing the French window behind him. A gust of wind blew in through the shattered glass.

'*You* killed my father,' Tanvi shouted, looking at Chauhan.

'That's absolute nonsense, Tanvi!' said Chauhan, outraged at the accusation, not to mention embarrassed, as a sizeable chunk of his staff were watching the scene by now.

'You are a murderer. I will kill you,' Tanvi continued.

'Please take her away,' Chauhan instructed the two burly security guards who had arrived at the cabin door. They walked over to Tanvi, lifted her off the ground without ceremony, and carried her out of the cabin and across the reception area towards the exit. Tanvi continued her tirade, hurling abuses and threats at Chauhan, who tried to maintain his composure as best he could.

Rohit was distraught. 'I am very sorry,' he said to Chauhan, before heading for the exit.

'It is okay, she is unwell. I understand,' Chauhan replied, adjusting his tie.

Bidding Chauhan a hurried goodbye, Aditya and Meera left. Aditya saw that the staff who had gathered to watch the spectacle had scattered by now. *Waiting for their coffee break to gossip about the boss*, he thought.

As they entered the elevator, Meera muttered to Aditya, 'She is crazy. Something must be done about her.'

She is right. Something must be done about Tanvi, Aditya concluded.

TWENTY—SEVEN

'**G**ood morning, Dr Mistry,' Aditya said, when she answered his call. He was driving to work the morning after the incident at Bakshi Pharma.

'Good morning, Inspector. Is everything fine with Tanvi and Rohit?' she asked.

Aditya described the previous day's events to Dr Mistry and asked for her opinion.

'It is uncommon, but quite possible, for persons in Tanvi's condition to drive a car. Most schizophrenics never forget certain skills that they acquired before the onset of their illness, that are essential for their functioning, like, say, walking. But they do develop selective memory about events and people, and are often delusional,' Dr Mistry explained.

Aditya thanked her, rang off and dialled Meera's number. 'Any news from Rohit?' he asked her.

'I spoke with him late last evening. After we dropped them off, there have been no developments.'

Aditya filled Meera in on his conversation with Dr Mistry.

'Don't you think the situation is getting increasingly dangerous for Rohit?' asked Meera.

'Yes, I agree,' Aditya conceded.

'It would be a shame if something were to happen to him,' Meera said.

TWENTY-EIGHT

Sam Mehta turned off the television at 2 a.m. and went to bed. He tossed and turned for a while but was unable to get a wink of sleep. Finally, he got up, put on his house-slippers and slowly made his way to the kitchen. He boiled a cup of water, dipped an Earl Grey tea bag into it and picked up the half-read book lying on the kitchen table. Then he went out to the patio, switched on the lights and sat down to read.

It was a quiet, moonless night; a large mass of clouds formed a blanket above, but a gentle breeze blew in from the sea. Sam felt himself relaxing. As he took the first sip from his cup, he heard the scream.

'Tanvi!'

It was Rohit's voice. Sam got up and hurried to the wall separating the two houses. At five feet six inches, he had to stand on his toes to look over the wall. He saw Tanvi walking slowly in the overgrown grass, in her white gown. Rohit was right next to her, calling out and waving his hands in front of her, but she did not seem to notice. Both of them had their backs to Sam.

Sam looked for a foothold in the wall, but there were none. He lowered himself and relaxed his legs for a few seconds before stretching up again. Rohit was now in front of Tanvi, facing his neighbour's wall, but too far for Sam to see him clearly.

Suddenly, Tanvi raised her hand. That was when Sam realised she was holding a knife. She brought it down as if to stab Rohit, who screamed and staggered backwards.

'Stop!' Sam shouted and ran out of his compound. He pushed open the iron grille of *Paradise* and ran along the driveway towards them. 'Rohit,' he yelled, as he saw Tanvi run back to the entrance. She pushed the front door open and disappeared into the house.

'Help,' he heard Rohit's faint voice. He was lying on his back, next to the tree. 'Are you all right?' Sam asked as he knelt down next to him. He was filled with relief when he saw that the knife had been thrust into the trunk of the tree. Sam helped Rohit get up, both of them out of breath. Rohit's face was white with fear.

'Thanks,' Rohit gasped, placing his hand on Sam's shoulder.

Both men stood in silence for the next few minutes, not knowing what to say or do. Then Rohit turned and started walking slowly back towards the house.

'Are you sure it is safe to go in now?' Sam asked.

'What choice do I have?'

'Should I call for help? Inspector Aditya, maybe?' Sam asked.

'How do you know him?' Rohit asked suddenly, and then said, 'Doesn't matter ... yes, please call him.'

Sam rushed back to his house. Rohit opened the door and stepped in.

TWENTY-NINE

When Aditya reached *Paradise* twenty minutes later, Sam was waiting at the gate. 'Thanks, Sam. I will take it from here,' Aditya said, much to the old man's relief.

A weary-faced Rohit had opened the door before Aditya reached the entrance. He waved Aditya inside and sat down on the sofa in the living room. The room was dimly lit and the television was on.

'What happened? How are you?' Aditya asked.

Covering his eyes with both hands, Rohit broke down and sobbed like a child. Aditya had never seen a grown man weep like this. He sat down next to Rohit, trying to console him. 'Everything will be okay.'

'I am sorry … I just …' said Rohit, embarrassed at his outburst.

'And where is Tanvi? How did you manage her?'

'I waited outside with Sam for some time. When I came back, she was in bed, sleeping, as if nothing had ever happened.'

'Come, let's see.' Aditya rose and went to the staircase, motioning to Rohit to follow him.

The door to Tanvi's room was ajar; a sliver of yellow light fell into the passage outside. Rohit whispered to Aditya, 'She must be awake again. I had switched off the light.'

They tiptoed to the door, slowly pushed it open and waited in the passage for a few seconds, listening for sudden movements inside. There were none. Aditya took a step inside.

'Who are you?' a calm voice inquired, startling both men. It was Tanvi. She was sitting on an armchair by the open window, its curtains swaying in the sea breeze.

'He … he is a friend … Aditya,' Rohit said.

'Hello, Aditya,' Tanvi said.

'Hello, Tanvi. How are you feeling now?' Aditya asked.

'I am fine. Why do you ask? Is something wrong with me?'

'No, not at all.'

'Now, if you will excuse me, I would like to sleep,' she said.

'Sure, goodnight,' Aditya said and turned back to the door.

'Goodnight, darling. Sleep well,' Tanvi said to Rohit, smiling slightly.

What game are you playing, Tanvi? Aditya wondered, as he walked out of the room.

THIRTY

'So, what do you make of it?' Aditya asked Meera the next day. They were having a cup of coffee after lunch.

'Can she plead insanity after committing a murder?' Meera asked.

'She could, given her current condition. But, wait a minute, are you saying Tanvi is *acting* ... that she wants to get Rohit out of the way for some reason?'

'I would not rule that out.'

Improbable though Meera's theory sounded at first, Aditya was impressed with her reasoning. *It is possible*, he conceded.

'But what could be her motive?'

'We will need to figure that out.'

In Aditya's head, the case suddenly assumed a completely new dimension. The possibility that Tanvi was putting up an act became an idea he simply could not get out of his head. He went over everything that had transpired in the case and its investigation—all the incidents, every single conversation and discussion—over and over again, but he found nothing to confirm or refute the theory. But whether Tanvi was acting or not, one fact could not be denied: Rohit's life was in danger. And Aditya decided to do something about it. He was not going to let another innocent life be destroyed, not on his watch.

That evening, after dropping Meera at her place, Aditya drove to *Paradise*. He was about to ring the bell when he saw that the door was partly open. Aditya stepped into the house and closed the door behind him. 'Rohit,' he called out. There was no answer. He looked in the kitchen; it was empty. 'Rohit,' he called again, a bit louder this time. Again, no answer.

He ran up the stairs and paused at the door to Tanvi's room, his hand on the cold steel knob. Not a sound. He turned the knob and pushed the door open. There was no one in the room. Although the sun had almost set, it was still bright enough for him to see clearly without having to switch on the lights. Aditya closed the door behind him and, on an impulse, opened the cupboard beside the bed and started going through its contents. Clothes, mostly home-wear, three white hospital gowns, bed linen and two towels. The bottom drawer contained worn-out footwear. He quickly went over to the mirrored wall cabinet and opened it. The cabinet had two shelves, with an array of medicines neatly arranged on them: two unused syringes, lying atop a boxful of them, and some tablets and vials.

Next, Aditya examined the bed; the wrinkled bedsheet was warm. On a hunch, he lifted the pillow. There it was. A brown-handled kitchen knife, with six inches of cold steel.

He picked the knife up and turned to leave. Tanvi stood at the door, staring at him. Aditya froze, unable to take his eyes off her, not knowing what to do. He hid his right hand, which held the knife, behind his back.

Tanvi looked through him with glassy eyes as she walked in, right past him. Aditya heaved an inward sigh of relief as he stepped back, letting her pass. She lay down on the bed and turned on her side, facing him. Then she closed her eyes. When he was convinced that Tanvi was asleep, he quietly left the room. On his way down, Aditya's thoughts returned to Rohit. *Where was he?*

Worried, he opened the front door and stepped out on the driveway, when he saw Rohit walk in through the gate. He was shabbily dressed in grey shorts and a loose polo-neck t-shirt, at least two sizes too big for him. Aditya wondered if it had fit him when he bought it.

Rohit waved to him. 'I was at Sam's,' Rohit explained, seeing the anxious look on Aditya's face.

'Come, let's take a walk,' Aditya said. 'Don't worry, she's still sleeping.'

He came straight to the point. 'Rohit, the nature of my job demands that I investigate a case from all angles, evaluating every possibility.'

'Yes, I get that. But what are you trying to say?'

'I have a few questions, if you are fine with answering them.'

'Sure, go ahead.'

'I understand that Bakshi Pharma is valued at over two thousand crores. What is the ownership structure?'

'Well, it is a public limited company. Tanvi, Chauhan and I own 45 per cent of the shares—15 per cent each. The rest is owned by public shareholders.'

'And if something were to happen to you, who gets your share?'

'Tanvi, obviously. But ... wait a minute, what are you implying?' Rohit was clearly agitated by the insinuation.

'I am not implying anything. As I just mentioned, it is my job to consider all possibilities.'

'Whatever you're thinking, it is ridiculous. Absolute rubbish!'

'Tell me one more thing. Before all this happened, who was Tanvi closest to?'

'Tanvi is an only child. She was very attached to her father, right from her childhood. Her mother passed away when she was thirteen. Probably that was why the shock of losing him so suddenly was devastating.'

'And ... who else?' Aditya asked.

'Tanvi was ... *is* ... a very private person. She hardly has any friends. Apart from her father, she was closest to me. She also relied a great deal on Chauhan in business matters.'

'And how was her personal equation with Chauhan?'

'Business aside, I don't think she liked Chauhan very much as a person. I believe she felt Chauhan was trying to sideline her.'

THIRTY-ONE

The doorbell rang. Aditya stirred and awoke; he saw that Meera was still fast asleep next to him. He got up and slowly walked to the door in the darkness, tripping over a pillow lying on the floor. He looked through the peephole, but could not see anyone. Then he opened the door; nobody was there. He stepped into the corridor. It was empty. He locked the door and climbed back into bed, putting his arms around Meera.

'Who was it?' she asked, stirring.

'Nobody,' Aditya said and opened his eyes as he realised that the voice did not belong to Meera. He turned towards the figure lying next to him. In the dim glow of the streetlight shining in through the window, he saw that the woman next to him was Tanvi. She had a strange smile on her face. He sat up on the bed with a start. Tanvi jumped up too, her eyes wild with excitement. Suddenly, with a swift motion of her hand, she pulled out a sharp, gleaming knife from under the pillow. And, with a piercing scream, she plunged the knife into Aditya's chest.

THIRTY-TWO

Aditya woke up with a jolt, soaked in cold sweat.
'What happened?' Meera asked, sitting up next to
him, holding his hand.

Aditya stood up, shuddering. It took him a few
seconds to register what had happened. Meera was
now standing next to him. She took him in her arms.
'It's okay. I am here.'

Aditya hugged her tightly. 'Don't leave me,' he
pleaded.

'I won't,' Meera said and led him back to bed. She
ran her fingers gently through his hair until he slept,
curled up like a child.

Aditya woke up the next morning to the aroma of
freshly brewed coffee. 'Good morning,' Meera said, as
she came into the bedroom with a steaming mug for
Aditya.

'Good morning,' he murmured, slightly embarrassed by the events of the previous night. Meera did not mention it, talking instead about their plans for the day ahead. He, too, quickly forgot about it.

'Why don't you freshen up? I'll have breakfast ready,' Meera said. Aditya smiled.

As they ate fried eggs and toast, Aditya held Meera's hand very tight. Meera looked at him quizzically, a slight smile on her face. Aditya was looking at the floor with an expression of deep concentration, as if trying to choose the right words. Finally, he said, 'Meera, I have a very serious question for you.'

'I am all ears.' She smiled at him.

'Will you marry me?'

'What! Are you serious, Mr Sachdev?'

'Never been this serious before. Will you marry me?'

'Yes, I will.' Meera blushed.

Aditya took her in his arms and held her close.

'I am so happy,' Meera said.

'I will go to Lucknow this very evening. My family will be thrilled to hear the news. We can then decide on a date for the wedding, after consulting your family.'

THIRTY-THREE

Pratap Chauhan stepped out of the posh apartment complex for his morning run. It was a daily routine he had not missed even once in eleven years. Irrespective of his schedule, and no matter how hectic his previous day had been, Chauhan would hit the road at 5 a.m. The sea-facing road in Worli was normally empty at this time of day, one of the reasons he preferred the early hour for his run.

Chauhan warmed up with a slow jog, a morning raga playing in his earphones. He picked up pace fifteen minutes later, as he approached the Bandra-Worli sea-link. He was feeling great; the run was invigorating and the music soothing.

The SUV followed him noiselessly at a distance of two hundred metres, headlights switched off. At the sea-link junction, Chauhan started to cross the road, to continue on his daily route. The SUV picked up speed and zoomed towards the running man. Chauhan, engrossed in his run, had reached the middle of the road when he saw the speeding car. He raised his hands, trying to signal to the driver to stop, but the SUV came straight at him.

The front bumper hit Chauhan with tremendous force, flinging him violently aside. His head struck the concrete divider before he hit the road, lifeless.

THIRTY-FOUR

Pratap Chauhan's prayer meeting was held at his Worli residence the next day. A large photograph of a smiling Chauhan, framed and garlanded, leaned against a wall in the spacious living room. Six chairs were lined up, three on either side of the photograph, the kind of seats usually reserved for family members of the deceased. Rohit and Tanvi occupied two chairs on one side. An old man who bore a striking resemblance to Pratap Chauhan was sitting on the third, next to Rohit. *Must be his elder brother*, thought Aditya. Three senior employees of Bakshi Pharma—Aditya recognised them from the day of Tanvi's violent episode in the office—were seated on the other side.

The room was filled with people. Aditya and Meera were seated next to Commissioner Gokhale, who had come to pay his respects, along with other grandees from the city administration as well as the corporate world. The attendance at his prayer meeting was ample testimony to the goodwill Chauhan had built over his lifetime.

Aditya was observing Tanvi. She was wearing a plain salwar-kameez and was looking down in distraction at her lap, fidgeting constantly. Rohit seemed sad and nervous, as always. From time to time, he exchanged a few words with the old man seated next to him. At one point, they both acknowledged the condolences offered by a guest with folded hands.

Gokhale turned to Meera and asked her softly, 'Meera, can you fill me in on the progress?' He gestured to her to step out. Aditya followed them, keen to get an update himself. He had been in Lucknow at the time of the accident, but cut his trip short on hearing the news and had returned the previous evening.

They descended the stairs from the first-floor apartment and approached a podium on the manicured front lawn. It was a windy evening, and for a moment, in spite of the grave circumstances that had brought them there, the trio could not help but admire the sun setting along the Arabian Sea, just across the road.

'Yes, Meera. Where are we on this?' Gokhale queried, after a pause.

'We have questioned the jogger who found Chauhan's body on the road. He had just started his run and did not see any vehicles around, so we could surmise that some time had elapsed since the accident.'

'Any other clue? Did anybody witness it from their balcony?' Gokhale asked.

'No, sir. We asked in all the neighbouring buildings.'

'What about CCTV cameras?' Aditya asked.

'Yes, we checked,' Meera said. 'Unfortunately, there is no CCTV at the junction where the accident occurred.'

'Hell!' Aditya punched his fists together.

'But I checked the cameras at the next signal. Before the accident, only one vehicle had turned towards this road yesterday morning. It was an SUV, probably dark brown or black.'

'Did we get the number plate and make of the SUV?' Aditya asked.

'We only got a side view of the vehicle when it made the right turn at the signal, so we couldn't capture the number plate. But the make of the car was discernible from the logo on the tyre plates. It was a Honda.'

THIRTY-FIVE

The morning after the prayer meeting, Aditya and Meera went to *Paradise*. As they got out of Aditya's car, they spotted Rohit seeing a middle-aged man off at the gate. The latter was dressed in a business suit and carried a leather briefcase. He shook hands with Rohit and walked to a silver Mercedes parked nearby, driving off by the time Aditya and Meera had crossed the road.

'Morning, who was he?' Aditya asked Rohit.

'Mahesh Sardesai, our family lawyer. He is also legal counsel for Bakshi Pharma,' Rohit said, leading them inside. As they walked down the driveway, Aditya's eyes were focused on the black Honda, which was parked in its usual spot. He glanced at Meera, who nodded slightly, as if she knew exactly what Aditya was thinking.

Aditya walked over to the Honda to inspect it. The damage was very visible; the front bumper was smashed and the right side of the bonnet, all the way down to the wing, was dented.

'What caused this?' Aditya asked Rohit.

Rohit hesitated for a moment before glancing up at the open window on the first floor. Aditya and Meera looked up, too, just in time to see Tanvi turning away from the window. *She was watching us,* Aditya realised.

'Actually, it was my doing ... I ran into a lamppost yesterday, while driving to the prayer meeting,' Rohit said, looking up at the window again. 'Come, let's go in.'

Rohit filled a couple of cups for them from the thermos flask on the table. As they sat sipping the lukewarm coffee, Rohit began, 'There is something you must know. Mahesh had come to deliver some news.'

Aditya and Meera leaned forward, waiting for him to continue.

'Remember I had told you that Chauhan, Tanvi and I—each of us—own 15 per cent of the shares in Bakshi Pharma?'

'I remember,' Aditya said.

'Mahesh looked after Chauhan's personal legal matters as well as ours. He was the executor of Chauhan's will. And ...'

'And?' Aditya asked, half-anticipating what Rohit was about to say.

'As per Chauhan's will, Tanvi is the sole beneficiary of his shares in Bakshi Pharma, effectively making her a 30 per cent owner in the company now.'

'What about his family?' Meera asked.

'Chauhan never married and has no close relatives, except an older brother who is also unmarried.'

'So Tanvi was the sole inheritor,' Meera said.

'Tell me, did Tanvi know she was the only beneficiary in Chauhan's will?' Aditya asked.

Just as Rohit was about to reply, they heard the familiar creaking sound. Tanvi was coming down the stairs.

Rohit whispered, 'Yes, she knew.'

THIRTY-SIX

'**D**o you think she murdered Chauhan?' Meera asked Aditya on their way back to Bandra Police Station.

'Well, the car that hit Chauhan was a dark-coloured Honda SUV. Tanvi owns one. And we know that she can drive, despite her condition. And now this—a three-hundred-crore motive! Too many coincidences. And I don't believe in coincidences.' Aditya shook his head.

'And she threatened Chauhan, that day at the office,' Meera reminded him.

'There you go. Makes my argument stronger.'

'Why don't we arrest her then?'

'On what basis? We have no solid evidence that Tanvi killed Chauhan. All the leads we had seem to converge at a dead end. Not to mention the fact that Rohit claims *he* crashed the car. And even if we were to prove somehow that Tanvi had a hand in Chauhan's death, she'll get away scot-free, given her condition.'

'If she is orchestrating all this, it is indeed a master-plot, but ...'

'But what?'

'Why is Rohit lying about the car?'

'Couldn't you see how terrified he was? If Tanvi had indeed driven the SUV out that morning to kill Chauhan, Rohit couldn't have been ignorant of the fact. And if he corroborates this, she will kill him. Not to mention the damage such a scandal would do to the reputation of the company,' Aditya reasoned.

'But he's missing the danger sign looming right in front of him. If Rohit dies, his 15 per cent stake will also go to Tanvi, and her share in the company would rise to 45 per cent,' Meera pointed out.

They drove in silence for the rest of the journey. *Cold-blooded, murderous bitch. Tanvi Acharya, you will not get away with this*, resolved Aditya.

Aditya was about to get out of the car at Bandra when Meera said, 'One of my closest friends is getting married in Pune next week. I am going there for a few days. Will you come with me? We can stay at my Pune apartment. It will be a welcome break; we both need it.'

'Sure, sounds good. I'll only be able to join you for a

couple of days, though. There is one more thing I have been meaning to tell you.'

'What?'

'After this case, we shouldn't work together … it's too much of a distraction for me.' Aditya smiled and winked. Meera blushed.

THIRTY-SEVEN

Aditya really enjoyed the Pune wedding. He reached the city on the morning of the wedding; Meera had arrived two days earlier. During the two days of celebrations that ensued, he saw a new side to Meera. She was the life of the party, cheerful and bubbly, and went out of her way to make Aditya feel comfortable, introducing him to all her friends as her fiancé. During his brief Lucknow visit, cut short by the unexpected death of Pratap Chauhan, he had spoken to his family about Meera. They were overjoyed to hear of his engagement, eager to meet Meera and her family at the earliest.

As the reception drew to a close, only family and a few close friends of the couple lingered at the venue, laughing and chatting. Meera sat next to Aditya, holding his hand. Aditya realised with a jolt of surprise that he had not thought about work at all since he had come to Pune. He could not remember when he had last laughed so much, without a care in the world.

He hugged Meera, whispering in her ear, 'Let's get married quickly.'

THIRTY-EIGHT

They finally left for Meera's apartment after 2 a.m. that night. After a twenty-minute drive on the Pune-Solapur highway, Aditya took a left, on Meera's directions, towards Hadapsar in eastern Pune. Once a small village, Hadapsar was now an upcoming industrial area with an ever-increasing population.

'I can hardly recognise this place,' Meera said, looking out at the burgeoning construction sites. 'Take a left here.'

Aditya turned into a narrow lane, just wide enough for a single vehicle, which led to a residential complex. The gate was closed. Aditya honked once to wake the security guard who was dozing in a small cabin by the entrance, and he came running to open the gate. Easing his Innova into the compound, Aditya saw four five-storeyed buildings, facing each other in pairs. There was a parking area on one side of the complex, and a small garden for children at the other end. Aditya parked in an empty slot.

Meera led him to a building labelled 'C Wing', and they took the stairs to her apartment on the third floor. It was a compact apartment that opened into a living room containing a red sofa and two chairs with matching upholstery. A narrow passage connected this room to the rest of the flat. There was a bathroom to the left of the passage and a kitchen to its right. It led to two adjoining bedrooms, one of which extended into a balcony where a two-seater wooden swing was suspended by metal chains.

'This is my favourite place in the house,' Meera said, referring to the swing, as she smiled at Aditya. 'I'll be back; make yourself at home.'

Aditya put his backpack on the floor in the bedroom next to the balcony and settled down in a rocking chair. His attention was drawn to a framed collage of photographs on the opposite wall. As he walked over to look at it, he tripped over a stool and upset a suitcase that had been placed on it. It was Meera's suitcase, the one she had brought to Pune with her; he remembered carrying it when he had dropped her off at the railway station earlier in the week.

'Oops,' he muttered, bending to pick it up. Not realising that the suitcase was unzipped, he lifted it by the handle, and its contents spilled out.

Meera came to the bedroom door, having heard the suitcase crash. Aditya was kneeling on the floor, trying to salvage the situation. 'Sorry,' he said to her, smiling sheepishly.

Meera took his hand. 'Let it be, we'll take care of that later. There are better things to do.' She smiled seductively and led him to the other bedroom.

THIRTY-NINE

Aditya woke at eight the next morning. He got up and walked out of the bedroom, looking for Meera. Hearing the faint squeaky sound of the swing, he made his way to the balcony. As he passed through the other bedroom, he noticed that Meera had cleared up the mess he had made and repacked the suitcase, which was now neatly stacked against the wall.

'Good morning,' said Meera cheerfully, sipping a cup of chai. She stopped the swing with her feet to let Aditya join her on it.

Aditya sat there for a few minutes, holding her hand, enjoying the peace and quiet of the morning. 'Let me get ready and start for Mumbai,' he said eventually, getting up reluctantly.

'Can you not stay another day?' Meera asked, taking both his hands in hers.

'I wish I could. But duty calls,' he said with a sigh.

Aditya left for Mumbai after a quick breakfast with Meera. 'I'll start back from here day after tomorrow. Drive safe,' she said, as she saw him off at the gate of her apartment complex.

As Aditya drove towards the Pune-Mumbai expressway, a sense of unease engulfed him. He could not quite put a finger on the reason for his discomfort, but something was bothering him. *Was Meera in any danger?* He had half a mind to turn back and stay another day with Meera. Reaching Bandra Police Station by lunchtime, he threw himself into his work but was unable to shake off the anxiety. *Stop worrying, nothing is going to happen*, he told himself.

FORTY

The day progressed very slowly for Aditya. He messaged Meera every thirty minutes or so, to check if she was all right. At 5 p.m., he had a meeting with Gokhale to discuss internal movements and promotions. He reached his superior's office a few minutes before the scheduled time.

'May I come in, sir?' Aditya asked, knocking on Gokhale's cabin door and opening it slightly.

'Please come in, Aditya,' Gokhale said. He called for tea, and they got down to business immediately. Ten minutes into the meeting, he asked Aditya, 'Are you all right? You seem to be preoccupied with something.'

'Nothing, sir. I am fine. Probably a bit tired, that's all.'

'Let's have this discussion some other day. Why don't you go home and get some rest?'

'I will take you up on that offer today, sir. Sorry about this. There's one other thing I wanted to talk to you about, though.'

'Sure, what is it?'

'I am getting married,' Aditya said, smiling slightly.

'Congratulations, my boy! That's excellent news. Who is the lucky girl?'

'Meera.'

'Meera Dixit?' Gokhale asked, and Aditya smiled and nodded. 'That's wonderful. I am delighted to hear this. So when is the big day?'

'Very soon, sir. Hopefully, the Acharya case will be solved soon. Immediately after that.'

FORTY-ONE

Aditya reached home at 7 p.m., much earlier than his usual time. Too tired to eat or change, he lay down on his bed, fully dressed. But his mind was still restless; he was thinking about Meera when he finally fell asleep.

He woke up to the sound of his mobile phone ringing. It was Rohit. He noted the time; it was 2 a.m.

'Aditya, please come quickly … she has gone berserk … she will kill me … please help me!'

'Calm down, Rohit,' Aditya said, wide awake now, but Rohit did not respond. The call was abruptly disconnected. Aditya tried Rohit's number again, but he did not pick up.

Aditya swiftly buttoned his shirt and put on his shoes. Picking up his handgun, a single-action Colt, he checked the chamber. Six bullets. Satisfied, he stuck the gun in its holster and sped out into the dark, moonless night.

He called Rohit again from the car phone, but there was no answer. *Pick up, pick up,* Aditya drummed impatiently on the steering wheel. He contemplated calling Meera, but decided against it. She was at least two hours away; there was nothing she could do.

At the Lilavati Hospital junction, he saw an ambulance speeding towards the hospital's emergency entrance. *Is that you, Rohit?* He reached for his phone again and called Rohit. No answer. 'Goddammit!' Aditya swore.

Carter Road was completely deserted, bathed in the orange glow of its street lamps. Lights were still on in a few houses. The sea was choppy; Aditya could hear the waves crashing furiously against the concrete breakers on the shore. His car screeched to a halt outside *Paradise* less than fifteen minutes after he had received Rohit's call. His eyes darted momentarily to Sam's house; all the lights were switched off.

As he approached the gate, he heard a scream, 'No, no ... don't!' It was Rohit's voice. He pushed the iron grille open and rushed in, just in time to see Rohit run into the house and Tanvi behind him, a glistening knife in her right hand, raised to strike.

Aditya removed his gun from its holster and

gripped it with both hands. He reached the front door, resolving to shoot it open if locked, but it was ajar. He could hear deafening music inside the house. The living room was completely dark, except for the flickering light of the television screen, where a music channel was playing *Sweet Child of Mine* at maximum volume. Aditya felt totally disoriented. He took two steps forward into the room, but stumbled on the small table by the sofas. As he regained his footing, he tried to create a mental map of the house from memory. He tried to recollect where the switchboard was but could not. A bead of sweat appeared on his forehead as he gripped the gun tightly, holding it in front of him.

'Help...' He heard Rohit's faint voice, which sounded like someone was choking him. Aditya's eyes followed the direction of the voice; it seemed to be coming from the far end of the room, but he could not be sure. Holding the gun in his right hand, he groped for some support with his left, but found none. As he stepped further away from the television, the faint, dancing rays from the screen cast a sinister, changeable light on the room. Aditya was concentrating hard, straining his ears to hear above the din of the music.

The voice again. 'Please ... don't.' *Help me, please. I don't want to die.* It was the voice of a man who knew his death was near.

Aditya frowned, trying to detect even the slightest

movement in the direction from where the voice came. Just then, a flicker of light from the television screen fell on a spot about thirty feet away and briefly illuminated the entwined bodies of Tanvi and Rohit, before fading again. They were in the dining area behind the large table, partially hidden by it. Rohit was lying flat on his back, squirming and twisting. Tanvi was on top of him, slowly forcing the knife down towards her husband's chest. Rohit was holding his wife's killer wrist, desperately trying to stop the knife from sinking fatally into him.

Standing in the darkness, gun in hand, Aditya deliberated. He realised he would have to take action. The blade was moving down swiftly, now barely a couple of inches from Rohit's trembling chest. He knew he was too far to reach Rohit in time to save him. Just then, the light flickered briefly on the two figures again. 'Aditya, help me!' Rohit screamed.

Aditya fired.

FORTY-TWO

For a few moments, Aditya was not sure what had happened. He felt his gun recoil, though only slightly, at the discharge; a flash of light seemed to go forth from his hand. He heard the deafening gunshot, amplified as *Sweet Child of Mine* faded to its conclusion in the same instant.

Aditya walked forward in a daze and felt a sticky liquid underneath the soles of his shoes as he approached the two bodies on the floor. Tanvi was lying motionless, face down in her hospital gown, on top of Rohit.

Aditya brought his gun forward again as he saw Tanvi's body move slightly. He then realised that it was Rohit trying to wriggle out from underneath her weight, using his outstretched palms for support. He was gasping for breath. 'Oh my God … oh my God,' he whimpered. Aditya pulled him out, dragging him through the pool of blood that was forming on the floor. Tanvi's lifeless body slid to the ground.

Aditya held Rohit by his shoulders to steady him, as his entire body was shaking violently. Leaning on him, Rohit limped towards the wall and switched on the lights. Aditya bent down to examine the scene.

Tanvi was stretched out on the floor, her dead eyes staring into nothingness. He could see the entry wound where the bullet had penetrated the right side of her neck; he realised it had killed her instantly. The blood flowing from her wound continued to dye her white hospital gown dark red and matted her long hair in its fast-congealing pool. Her right hand still refused to let go of the deadly knife.

Rohit was now squatting on the floor, holding his head in his hands. Aditya sat down next to him, wrapping an arm around him. Rohit wept inconsolably, streams of tears flowing down his sunken cheeks. He looked at Aditya with an expression that conveyed both grief and gratitude. Aditya suspected he also saw a hint of anger flare up briefly in the other man's eyes. *After all*, he reminded himself, *I just shot and killed his wife.*

FORTY-THREE

Aditya found the remote on one of the sofas and switched off the television, which was now playing Led Zeppelin's version of *Killing Floor*. Rohit was still sitting on the floor, sobbing. Aditya pulled out his phone and dialled his subordinate at the Bandra Police Station. He explained the situation briefly and gave him the address. 'Get an ambulance too,' he instructed.

His head was reeling as he sat down on the sofa. He had just killed somebody. A civilian. A woman. *But what if you had not fired the shot?* he asked himself. *You have saved a life. Prevented a cold-blooded murder.*

He was still grappling with his emotions when he heard the sirens. He went to the door; Rohit, too, was by his side when he let the police in. Among them, he recognised Sub-Inspector Apte from the WTC incident.

'Sir.' Apte saluted Aditya.

Aditya acknowledged him with a brief handshake and realised that, for the first time in his life, his hands were unsteady. 'Take my statement once you're through with the formalities,' he told Apte.

'Yes, sir. We are waiting for the ambulance.'

Aditya then called Gokhale and informed him of what had happened. 'I will be there right away,' Gokhale said. Next, he dialled Meera's number. She picked up on the fourth ring.

'Hey, what's up? All okay? It's three-thirty in the morning!' she said.

'I ... I shot her,' Aditya managed to say. Then, without warning, his breathing became shallow, and he felt as if he was in a daze, his emotions strangely benumbed.

'Aditya, talk to me. Are you all right? Is Rohit okay?' Meera sounded anxious.

'I killed her, Meera,' Aditya said.

'I am on my way. You hang in there,' Meera said and disconnected the line.

Aditya was in the courtyard when he made the call to Meera, and Rohit was standing next to him. The two men looked at each other, drained out and unable to speak or move, but each offered his silent support to the other. The quiet was broken by the wailing siren of the ambulance. The white van, its blue lights blazing, sped up along the driveway and halted right next to the two men. Four paramedics jumped out of the van, two of them carrying a stretcher.

Apte led the paramedics into the house. Rohit followed them in. Aditya waited outside. He saw the lights go on in Sam's cottage; the old man appeared at *Paradise's* gate a few minutes later.

'What happened?'

Aditya told him.

'God bless her soul.'

It was around 4 a.m. when Gokhale drove in. He walked up to Aditya, patted him on his shoulder and said, 'Don't worry. We will manage this.' He then proceeded to the house, where Apte and his team were securing the scene before the body was taken away.

The police photographer was taking pictures when Gokhale approached the spot where Tanvi's body lay. All the men working on the scene ceased their activity and stood to attention on seeing the Commissioner. He acknowledged them and said sternly, 'Not a word of this to the media. I will call for a press conference myself tomorrow; but until then, not a word goes out. Is that understood?'

'Yes, sir,' his subordinates said in unison.

Gokhale indicated to the waiting paramedics to get on with their jobs. Two of them lifted and strapped Tanvi's body to the stretcher. They walked briskly out of the house towards the ambulance parked in the garden. The other two paramedics led the way, opening the doors of the van and climbing in. They then helped their colleagues with the stretcher, which was placed on a narrow bed in the back of the van. Rohit climbed in after them and occupied a seat by the bed. Aditya stood by the back door and looked at Rohit, who seemed to have regained a bit of his composure. He sat quietly, staring at Tanvi's lifeless body. The inside of the van resembled an emergency room, stocked with medical equipment, monitors and oxygen tanks.

None of that will be of any use today, Aditya thought as he watched the ambulance speed away.

FORTY-FOUR

It was almost 6 a.m. when Aditya returned to Bandra Police Colony. It was a beehive of activity already, bustling with policemen who were leaving for work or returning from duty. Some residents were jogging in the small park inside the complex; others relaxed on the benches, chatting. The early rays of the sun were cutting through a metallic sky, promising a sunny day.

But for Aditya, the cold, hostile night persisted. He felt that all eyes were on him—questioning, accusing him. He could hear their murmurs as he passed. Maybe he was imagining it, he told himself, but it was still unsettling. The news would soon spread; of that, he was certain. He felt completely drained, both physically and emotionally.

He was slowly climbing the stairs to his second-floor apartment when he heard hurried footsteps behind him.

He turned around to see Meera running up towards him. He hoped she would hug him. She did.

'I am so glad to see you,' he said, holding her tight.

'So am I. Come, let's go up and you can tell me everything.'

As soon as they entered his apartment, Aditya slumped onto a chair, exhausted. 'Let me make some tea; then we can talk,' Meera said, going into the kitchen. Ten minutes later, she came out with two steaming cups and placed them on the small dining table. Aditya sat down opposite her and took a sip from his cup. He felt himself relaxing almost instantly.

'What a crazy night!' he exclaimed. Meera was silent, waiting for him to talk. Aditya narrated everything that had happened, right from the time he left her house in Pune. The nameless anxiety he had felt along the way. Rohit's distress call. Aditya's response. The scene he had walked in on, at *Paradise*. And finally, the shooting. Meera poured Aditya a second cup as he spoke.

He went over every single point in minute detail. Meera listened without interrupting, partly because she was deeply involved in the case and partly because she wanted Aditya to get it off his chest. She knew what was bothering Aditya most of all—the terrible question of whether he had taken the right call when he fired the fatal bullet.

'You did the right thing, Aditya,' Meera said when Aditya reached the end of his account. 'You did *absolutely* the right thing. You saved Rohit's life.' She hugged him warmly. Aditya smiled at her; it was just the reassurance he needed.

'What now? What will happen next?' Meera asked after a while.

'You mean … with me?' Aditya asked.

'Yes, how will the department take it?'

'That remains to be seen. I will speak to …' Aditya trailed off as his phone rang. It was Gokhale.

'Morning, sir,' Aditya said.

'I am calling for a press conference at Headquarters at noon today. Please be there,' Gokhale said.

'Yes, sir.'

FORTY-FIVE

Commissioner Hemant Gokhale walked in for the media briefing exactly at the stroke of noon. He was accompanied by the Deputy Commissioner, Aditya and Meera. The media relations officer of the police department was already in the room, speaking with a senior journalist from a leading daily. The room was buzzing; around fifteen reporters were seated at the massive conference table, with iPads and laptops. Some of them were already adding finishing touches to their 'stories', preparing to email their article the moment the briefing was over. Among them was a solitary old journalist who sat calmly with notebook and pen in hand, making for a very rare sight.

The police team sat at one end of the table, Gokhale at its head. The room fell silent as the Commissioner settled down and began his briefing. It was evident that everyone expected a big, juicy piece of breaking news.

'Good afternoon, ladies and gentlemen,' said Gokhale. 'We have been working on a very complicated and delicate case over the last few months. It concerned the safety—rather, the very survival—of an innocent and respectable citizen of Mumbai. And for our department, the safety of our citizens, *your* safety, is of paramount importance.'

Aditya was impressed with the way Gokhale opened the meeting. He understood that the Commissioner was preparing the ground for his defence, and the department as a whole, against the severe backlash that would inevitably follow. It was the age of media sensationalism, and Aditya was certain that the press would have a field day once they had heard the Commissioner. He shuffled restlessly in his chair, bracing for the impending volley of questions. Meera looked at him and smiled. *Everything will be all right*, she seemed to convey.

For the next twenty minutes, Gokhale spoke, almost uninterrupted, as the media took notes furiously. 'That's all I had to say. We can take questions now, if any,' he concluded.

A dozen hands went up simultaneously, and the room erupted into complete chaos. Gokhale raised both his hands, as if to ask for a semblance of order. Then he pointed to a female reporter whom he recognised from earlier briefings, indicating that they would take her question.

'Was it really necessary to shoot a woman, especially one who was unwell—both physically and mentally?' She addressed Aditya directly.

Gesturing to Gokhale that he was fine with taking the question, Aditya said, 'I feel terrible about shooting her. But I had to do what I did to save another life. Tanvi Acharya would undoubtedly have killed her husband if I hadn't fired that shot.'

'But if Tanvi Acharya was so sick, why wasn't she admitted to a hospital?' another journalist asked.

'That was the wish of the family—to take care of her at home, despite her mental state,' Aditya replied.

'You also recently shot a man at the World Trade Centre. Has this become an irresponsible and dangerous habit, Inspector Sachdev?' It was the woman who had asked Aditya the first question. The other reporters backed her up, demanding an explanation from Aditya and the police department, creating quite a furore.

Gokhale could see the situation slip out of their hands, as Aditya fumbled for an answer. 'We are here for your safety,' Gokhale finally interjected, 'and for that, we will do whatever it takes. Thank you for your time.' He stood up, indicating that the briefing was over, and left the room along with his team. The media relations officer tried to calm the journalists down but the uproar continued; its sounds pursued Aditya as he walked down the corridor.

FORTY-SIX

The media went on a rampage over the shooting of Tanvi Acharya. The news made headlines on television channels and in the newspapers. Various parties demanded the resignation of Commissioner Hemant Gokhale and Superintendent of Police Aditya Sachdev. The National Human Rights Commission and other activists staged a protest outside the Mumbai Police Headquarters and marched from there to the Chief Minister's bungalow on Malabar Hill. The pressure on the police department only intensified as the days went by.

A fortnight had passed since the shootout. Aditya was sitting in Gokhale's office. He was unshaven, had barely eaten in the past weeks and appeared to have aged a few years in a matter of days. The dark circles under his eyes and his drooping eyelids indicated he had not slept, possibly since the night he had shot Tanvi. Meera was sitting next to him, looking much more in control of herself.

They were waiting for Gokhale to return from his meeting with the Chief Minister. It was the first time that they had ever known Gokhale to be late for a scheduled meeting. He finally arrived thirty minutes past the appointed time, gave them a curt nod and sat down. He looked at Aditya with a pained expression in his eyes. The young officer was one of his favourites, and he hated to see him like this.

'Well,' Gokhale began, 'I met the Chief Minister today to discuss the next steps in this case.'

'And what did he say?' Meera asked. Aditya kept his eyes on the floor.

'As you know, there is tremendous pressure from all sides to take action. The media, human rights organisations, citizen associations ... and of course, politicians. But there is good news ...' Gokhale said, his expression still grim.

Aditya did not look up even then. It was Meera who said, 'What is it, sir? Please tell us.'

'The good news is that it can be conclusively proven that Aditya shot Tanvi to save Rohit's life. The testimony supporting this claim can be given by you,' Gokhale pointed towards Meera, 'and Rohit. So, chances are that no criminal proceedings will be initiated against Aditya. As you know, a criminal investigation can only proceed on evidence; all evidence in this case proves that Aditya did what was right—saving the life of a defenceless, innocent citizen. But ...'

Meera braced herself for the bad news; she had known from the start that something was wrong, judging from Gokhale's facial expressions. Aditya now slowly looked up and, without saying a word, stared at Gokhale, waiting for the final blow.

'But,' Gokhale continued, 'there will be a departmental enquiry. We *have* to take some action, although it will just be for the sake of optics, I'm sure. I am hoping the department will take a fair view of what has happened.' He looked at Aditya, who had once again lowered his eyes. Slowly, he and Meera rose and started for the door.

'The enquiry will commence tomorrow,' the Commissioner said.

FORTY-SEVEN

The departmental enquiry lasted six weeks. Aditya was questioned for at least four hours every day, and the committee deliberated endlessly. Meera, too, was asked to depose before the committee. Initially, she had moved in with Aditya to take care of him. However, three weeks into the proceedings, Aditya's parents came from Lucknow, and Meera went back to her apartment. She was at Aditya's place virtually all the time, however, and got along very well with his family. Aditya was tense and distraught; he had lost a lot of weight and his face looked haggard. He could not bring himself to focus on anything other than the outcome of the enquiry. The family did everything they could to keep him in good spirits, but their efforts were futile.

Rohit visited Aditya's home frequently, to extend his support. 'I cannot thank you enough, Aditya. Please let me know if I can be of any help,' he said warmly on every occasion.

It was a Monday afternoon. The enquiry commission was set to announce its verdict the following day. Meera was sitting with Aditya and his parents in his living room when her phone rang. 'Hello,' she said, and listened intently for the next few minutes, her expression conveying increasing panic. 'I will leave immediately,' she said, as she hung up.

'What happened? Is everything okay?' Aditya asked.

'My father ... he had a heart attack this morning. His condition is critical. I have to leave ...' Meera said, bursting into tears.

'Oh my God,' Aditya said, as he held Meera's hands. 'I will go with you.'

'No, no ... you have to be here tomorrow. I will let you know how things are ... then we can decide what to do.'

Aditya agreed reluctantly. 'Let me drive you to the airport at least. Do you need to go home first?'

'No, I will go directly to the airport. I just want to see Baba,' Meera said, teary-eyed.

Aditya dropped her at the airport and drove back home, his mind filled again with thoughts of the following day. It was around 11 p.m. when Meera called him. 'Hey, everything is fine. He had a mild attack, but he is much better now.'

'Thank God for that,' Aditya said, relieved.

'He'll be in the hospital for two days, after which we will shift him home. But I'll stay here for a week to take care of him. Is that okay?'

'Of course, you must stay with him.'

'I wish I could've been there for you tomorrow. You take it easy ... okay? You have done nothing wrong.'

'Yes, don't worry. I will call you after ... I know what the decision is,' Aditya said.

'I am so sorry, Aditya. Wish I was there with you,' Meera said again, as she hung up.

FORTY-EIGHT

On Tuesday, Aditya reached the Police Headquarters fifteen minutes before the verdict was due to be announced. He went to see Gokhale but was told that the Commissioner was already in the meeting room with the members of the enquiry committee. Aditya hovered near the entrance of the meeting room where a uniformed constable sat on a chair by the closed door. He glanced at his watch; it was past the scheduled time but the door did not open. Another fifteen minutes went by; Aditya was getting impatient, pacing nervously in the corridor. He asked the constable what was going on, but the man shrugged his shoulders.

Twenty minutes later, the door opened. A uniformed sub-inspector emerged and asked Aditya to go in. In the room, Aditya saw the three members of the enquiry committee seated at the head of the table. Gokhale sat next to them, to the left. The only other people in the room were the sub-inspector who had let him in and a lawyer employed by the department. The sub-inspector was recording the minutes of the meeting and the lawyer was present to ensure that the proceedings did not violate the Constitution.

'Have a seat,' one of the committee members told Aditya, pointing to a chair on their right. Aditya sat down, looking at the members and then at Gokhale. The Commissioner's expression revealed nothing.

'We have concluded our enquiry, which included discussions with yourself, your colleagues and your seniors, Commissioner Gokhale included.' The committee member continued, 'We have also extensively reviewed previous cases and judgements. However, I must say, this is the first time that we are faced with a case that is so nuanced. So, what we are about to pronounce will also be a landmark judgement.'

Aditya straightened up in his seat. The sub-inspector passed around a dossier, containing copies of relevant documents and evidence for each of the attendees. Aditya looked at the thick stack of papers in front of him in a daze. The committee then went on to describe the incident, the circumstances of the case and the details of the police investigation as well as of their own enquiry, frequently referring to specific pages in the set of documents. The committee took longer than an hour to deliver their full report.

'And after due consideration to the matter, we have reached a unanimous verdict.'

Aditya looked at Gokhale, who turned away as soon as his eyes met Aditya's. *He knows*, Aditya realised.

The committee president pronounced his verdict, 'Aditya Sachdev, your service to the nation and the police force has been exemplary. And this is a fact we have considered before arriving at our decision. However, as a police officer in your position, you are required to maintain absolute integrity while discharging your duties. The shooting and killing of a woman who was mentally ill was a violation of the code of conduct that the department abides by. We note that no order sanctioning such act was issued by your superiors, either in writing or orally.' There was a pause as the president turned a page. Aditya rolled his eyes. *Orders from superiors, when a life hangs in the balance and a split-second decision has to be made ... give me a break.*

The president continued, 'The committee finds your behaviour reckless, and given the enormity of the outcome, we find there is more than sufficient ground for dismissal from service.'

To Aditya, the rest of the meeting was a blur, as he stared at Gokhale in complete disbelief. *Dismissal from service.* He took enormous pride in being part of the police force; it gave his life meaning and purpose. And the dishonour of being thus dismissed could not be worse if he had been stripped naked in public. His vision was hazy, he realised, due to the tears in his eyes; his head reeled and he had to hold on to the arms of his chair to keep from falling out of it.

'… the judgement will be effective immediately,' the president of the committee pronounced. The committee then left the room. Gokhale walked up to Aditya and put his hand on his shoulder. 'I am sorry, Aditya. I did my best.'

FORTY-NINE

Aditya changed in the locker room and left the Police Headquarters after surrendering his uniform, a set of keys to his office and the keys to his Innova. His gun had already been confiscated, right after the shooting. He had been asked to vacate his quarters in a week. He hailed a cab and dialled Meera's number as he got in. Her phone was switched off. *She must be in the hospital*, he thought.

He reached home and broke the news to his parents, who were devastated. Aditya tried Meera's number again, but it was still unreachable. 'Please call me asap,' he messaged her and went for a shower. He came out and immediately checked his phone. There were two new messages, both from subordinates who expressed their regret over the committee's decision, which they thought was grossly unfair. There was no reply from Meera yet.

'Don't worry, son. Everything happens for the best. We are very proud of you,' his father said, as he sat down next to Aditya.

'Why don't you come to Lucknow with us for a few days? It will do you good, away from all this ... and Meera is also not here for a week,' Aditya's mother suggested.

'That is a great idea. Start packing,' his father said. Aditya nodded, still looking at his phone.

The week in Lucknow did Aditya a world of good. He was away from the media glare; and more importantly, he spent some quality time with his family after years. Most of all, he enjoyed spending time with his niece, playing with her, driving her to school, taking her on bicycle rides. *Maybe it's all for the best*, he thought.

But the lack of contact with Meera was worrying him. *Has something happened to her father? Or is she in any trouble?* For her, he wanted to return to Mumbai; he decided to do so after eight days.

He headed straight from the Mumbai airport to Azad Maidan Police Station.

FIFTY

'Good morning, sir,' Constable Salunkhe saluted Aditya as he walked in.

Aditya smiled at him and said, 'No need to salute now, Salunkhe. I am no longer in service. Where is Meera?'

'Meera madam came here two days back. She was very disturbed. She said she has resigned from the police force.'

'What? Resigned? What are you saying?' Aditya could not believe what he was hearing.

'That is what she told me, sir. She cleared her locker and left.'

'Did she say anything about where she was going? Did she leave a message for me?' Aditya asked.

'No, sir. I've told you everything I know. But she told me that she met Commissioner Gokhale before she came here.'

Aditya left immediately and reached the Police Headquarters in less than five minutes. He strode up to the Commissioner's room. Fortunately, Gokhale was in his office.

'Aditya, how are you? Come in,' he said.

'Sir, did Meera come here?' Aditya asked impatiently.

'Yes, she did come here a couple of days back. She told me that ... after what had happened with you, she could not continue in this line of work. She was very depressed, I could make out. She tendered her resignation, and given her state of mind, I thought it was best to accept it. This case has claimed one more casualty, Aditya.'

'I am very worried about her as well, sir. I have been trying to call her for a week, but I can't reach her on her phone.'

'Yes, she did mention that there was some problem with her phone.' Gokhale frowned.

'I will go to her apartment,' Aditya said, turning to leave.

'She has already vacated her police quarters and handed the keys over to admin yesterday. She might have gone to Pune,' Gokhale said.

'Or Kolhapur. To her parents. Sir, can you have someone dig out her Kolhapur address from the records and ask the local police there to check on her? I will speak to the Hadapsar station officer and ask him to go to her Pune flat. I am really worried, sir,' Aditya said.

'Sure, Aditya. I will work on her Kolhapur address. Keep me posted. I am worried about her too.'

FIFTY-ONE

Aditya's phone buzzed after three hours. It was the Hadapsar station officer. 'Hello, officer. What is the update?' asked Aditya.

'Sir, we went to the address you gave us, but Meera Dixit's flat is locked. We enquired with her neighbour, who informed us that she went there last week and left the following day.'

'Left? Where? Did you get any details?'

'The neighbour saw her leave the flat with three large suitcases. We don't have any more details, sir.'

'Okay, thank you for your help,' Aditya hung up.

Aditya was about to dial Gokhale's number when his phone rang again. It was Gokhale. *Please give me some positive news*, Aditya prayed silently as he answered the call.

'Yes, sir.'

'Aditya, we should have an update from Kolhapur any moment now. Why don't you come over to my office later so we can discuss this?' Gokhale said.

'Sure, sir. I will be there.'

FIFTY-TWO

'May I come in, sir?' Aditya stood at the Commissioner's door.

'Come in, Aditya. Sit down.' Gokhale's expression was serious.

'What is the matter, sir?'

'Aditya, listen to me very carefully. Our station officer at Kolhapur went to the address we have on our records for Meera,' Gokhale said and paused.

'And?'

'Meera's family does not live there. That address belongs to someone else.'

'What? That's not possible ... there has to be a mistake. Her father suffered a heart attack last week, and she went home to Kolhapur.' Aditya was completely bewildered.

'We checked, Aditya. And ... her parents died when she was eleven. She was raised in a foster home in Pune.'

FIFTY-THREE

Aditya's head was pounding as he left Gokhale's office. *What are you up to, Meera? Where are you?*

He dialled Meera's phone again as he went down the stairs. It was switched off. He hailed a taxi outside the Police Headquarters and climbed in, still lost in thought.

'Sir, where to?' the cabbie asked.

'Bandra East,' Aditya replied.

As the taxi approached Peddar Road, Aditya's phone buzzed again. Hoping it was Meera, Aditya checked it immediately. It was Dr Mistry.

'Hello, Inspector,' she said.

'Hello, Dr Mistry.' Aditya did not bother to correct the salutation.

'Can we meet at my clinic? I have some information that may be vital to your case.'

'Now?'

'Now.'

FIFTY-FOUR

Thirty minutes later, Aditya was seated opposite Dr Mistry at her clinic.

'So, Doctor, you said you had some important information to share?'

'Yes, I think so,' she started, looking at Aditya, 'I was in Germany for almost two months, and completely out of touch with what was happening here. I came back last night and heard about everything that has gone down.'

Aditya nodded, eager to hear what Dr Mistry had to say.

She continued, 'I read about Tanvi trying to kill Rohit, and the unfortunate incident in which she lost her life. Something struck me as extremely odd; that is what I want to discuss with you.'

'Odd? Go ahead, please,' Aditya said, leaning forward.

'The night Tanvi died, at around 9 p.m., I received a call from her. She sounded very disturbed; I put it down to Mr Chauhan's death. She pleaded with me to visit her but told me specifically not to tell Rohit that I was coming over. I think she wanted to tell me something. So, I reached her residence at around half-past nine. Rohit was clearly surprised—shocked, rather—to see me. He seemed very nervous for some reason.'

Aditya was on the edge of his chair, unable to bear the suspense.

'When I told Rohit I was there to see Tanvi, he said she was fast asleep and did not want to be disturbed. I insisted on seeing her and went up to her room, despite Rohit's protests. Tanvi was sleeping. I tried to wake her up, but could not. That's when I realised she had been injected with a very strong sedative. Then, I saw her right arm and all those syringe marks ... the countless times she was subjected to—' Dr Mistry's voice faltered.

She gathered herself with an effort and said, 'It was inhuman, the way she was being treated. I had prescribed the sedative in the event of extreme emergencies, but it was evident that she was being administered injections very frequently. So I confronted

149

Rohit. When I threatened to take drastic action, he broke down and said he was forced to use the sedatives daily because of her violent episodes, which were becoming more frequent. But somehow, I had trouble believing him; so many injections were unnecessary, under any circumstances. I suspected that something was amiss and insisted that Tanvi be moved to a nursing home immediately. Rohit agreed at once; he promised he would move her to a hospital the very next day. Satisfied with his reply, I left. The same night, I left for Germany.'

'Okay, so Tanvi was being sedated very frequently— maybe daily, perhaps more than once a day—with heavy doses that were unwarranted. In fact, Doctor, I suspected as much, too,' Aditya sighed.

'Yes, that's correct. But you're missing the main point, Inspector,' Dr Mistry said.

'And that is?'

'My point is, that night, Tanvi was drugged so heavily that it would have been impossible for her to get out of bed on her own, let alone attack Rohit.'

FIFTY-FIVE

'**B**ut that's impossible,' Aditya protested. 'I saw her. She would have killed Rohit if I had not fired. She was pushing the knife down …' Aditya stopped himself mid-sentence. *Rohit was holding Tanvi's wrist. Was he really defending himself or … pretending? Had Rohit been acting all along?* Aditya began thinking about that night from a completely different perspective.

If Tanvi could not move of her own volition, as Dr Mistry had pointed out, Rohit must have positioned his sedated wife on top of himself, also propping the knife in her right hand. He was not pushing it away; he was, in fact, pretending to bring it down towards himself. Tanvi was not trying to kill Rohit; she couldn't have. The darkness, with its dancing lights, and the loud music, completed the illusion. Masterminded by Rohit.

He grasped the arms of the chair and stiffened, a cold dread hitting him like a punch in the gut. Head spinning, he reached out with shaky hands for the glass of water on Dr Mistry's table. He gulped it down, spilling some on himself, and put the glass down, feeling nauseated. Rushing out without a word to Dr Mistry, he hurried to the restroom next to the reception. He retched, gasping for air, then splashed water on his face, ran his hands through his hair and looked at himself in the mirror. He shook his head slowly, as a wave of anger and disbelief overcame him.

Impossible for her to get up ... but then, who did he see running after Rohit that night?

He was walking back to Dr Mistry's office, when he heard the siren of an ambulance. His mind went back to the day he left Meera's house after the wedding in Pune—that feeling of unease, of something bothering him. *What was it?* And then it hit him. It had been staring him in the face all along. But he had missed it.

That night, at Meera's house, when her suitcase accidentally opened and the contents spilled out, he had caught a glimpse of it. It had fallen to the floor, partly hidden between two other dresses.

A white hospital gown.

That was it! What was bothering him that day, triggering that nameless anxiety. The hospital gown.

In Meera's suitcase. *But that meant* ... Aditya was shaking violently as he drew the inevitable conclusion ... *it was not Tanvi he had seen running after Rohit, it was Meera! She must have left for Mumbai immediately after he left from Pune and reached Paradise.*

Meera and Rohit were in it together!

The stage had been set perfectly, and Aditya was the unwitting actor.

Aditya, help me! A voice from the past spoke in his head again. And then, he heard the gunshot.

Aditya came back to the present with a shudder.

FIFTY-SIX

Six months had passed since Aditya's revelation at Dr Mistry's clinic. Unable to stay in Mumbai, he had moved back to Lucknow. Aditya was a changed person now, inside and out. He had shrunk; his once erect frame slouched when he walked, and his wild hair was more grey than black. He had a perpetual scowl, as if he was upset with himself. And would remain so. Forever.

Every night, Aditya stayed awake, sitting on his armchair, staring into empty space. He had no thought of what to do the next day, no plans for the life ahead. *If at all there is a life,* he thought. *Well, my plan is to sleep, for a while, at least. Is that too much to ask for? Please … let me sleep …* he seemed to be pleading with an invisible entity.

In his mind, he played out the events of the case over and over again. Every time, he would imagine a course of action different from the one he had taken. And each time, he would imagine a different outcome. An outcome that would let him sleep peacefully. An outcome that would let him live. With himself.

What if I had not accepted the assignment?
What if I had not fired that night?
What if I had not fallen in love?

EPILOGUE

One year later

It was 7.30 p.m. The affluent town of Kilchberg, on the silver coast of Zurich, was quiet on that cold winter night. She stood in the garden of a two-storeyed villa, her slim figure clad in denims and a green cardigan, watching the sun slowly disappear over Lake Zurich.

She took another sip of coffee and looked down at the week-old Indian newspaper she was holding. She turned to page two and read the headlines again, as she had done several times over the past days, as if to confirm that they had not changed with time.

But *she* had. The thought caught her unawares. She shook her head; no, she had not *changed*. It was as if her earlier self did not exist, ever. The one who joined the police force for the right reasons. The one who wanted to live a straightforward, honest life. She could not remember when that Meera Dixit had died. Or who killed her. Maybe she had, herself.

The chance encounter with Rohit in the first year of her posting in Mumbai. And then, life—or rather, death—took its own course. Love spawned overriding greed and ambition. And a lack of remorse. Tanvi's illness presented the opportunity; careful preparation and planning did the rest. And Aditya, the perfect fall guy, completed the plot by pulling the trigger.

She did not notice Rohit come out into the garden with a can of beer, until he was standing next to her, his arm around her. Meera said nothing.

As if reading her mind, he asked, 'Any regrets?'

She gently touched his left shoulder, at the exact spot where a faint scar still remained. 'Only this,' she said.

Rohit took the newspaper from her hand, his eyes caressing the headline again: *Violet Pharma buys Rohit Acharya's 45 per cent stake in Bakshi Pharma for 900 crores.*

'We have done it,' he chuckled.

She smiled and kissed him.

Made in the USA
Middletown, DE
12 September 2020

19327051R00099